BACA

BACA
A Ronny Baca Novel
By
Billy Kring

Copyright © 2014

ALL RIGHTS RESERVED

This is a work of fiction. Names, characters, businesses, organizations, places, events, and incidents either are the product of the author's imagination or are used fictitiously. Any resemblance to actual persons, living or dead, events, or locales is entirely coincidental.

ISBN: 978-1499644371

Cover Image by:
Elizabeth Mackey Graphic Design, *www.elizabethmackey.com*

For my talented and crazy-fun friends in the entertainment industry.

Mystery/Suspense by Billy Kring
The Hunter Kincaid series
Quick
Outlaw Road

Romantic Suspense
(As B.G. Kring)
Where Evil Cannot Enter

CHAPTER ONE

I sat at my desk in a tee shirt and shorts, cooling down after a workout at the gym next door and checking the internet for any open casting calls so I could have my ego crushed again. That's when a Milla Jovovich clone, wearing big diamonds and a criminally short white skirt walked into my office.

"Ronald Baca?" she asked as she sat in the chair across from my desk.

"You've got me."

She looked me over and said, "You don't look Hispanic."

"Ancestors were from Bolognia. It's over near Spain."

She didn't blink. "Mr. Baca, my name is Bond Meadows, and I need to hire you." Bond crossed her legs and I looked at flawless tanned skin on two long legs. Her face and the name were vaguely familiar.

I said, "What would this be about Ms..."

"Mrs."

"Okay, Mrs. Meadows?"

She said, "I want you to find someone."

"Someone you'd like to locate or someone missing?"

"Missing."

"Have you filed a report with the police?"

"No, it's not like that. Maybe you've heard of him, Robert Landman?"

"The actor?" I'd heard of him. So had most of the planet. Landman was in the league of Brad Pitt and George Clooney, where attaching his name to a movie almost guaranteed good box office. I said, "What makes you think he's missing?"

"My husband is Frank Meadows, head of Americas Studios, and Bob is working there."

I knew of Meadows. Frank's unofficial nickname around town was "Fat Man" Meadows, as in the name of the second atomic bomb. It had to do with the record number of box-office mushroom clouds that his studio had sent to the viewing public over the last two years. No one called Frank "Fat Man" to his face, though. Frank had the reputation as a legitimate tough guy who enjoyed the company of ex-cons and not-so-ex-cons.

Frank's name made me remember where I'd seen this woman. It was in the society columns, with her husband. Something else about her was worming around in my skull, but I couldn't bring it forward.

She said, "Bob's not at home, and he's not on location filming. He left no forwarding information and I haven't heard from him in three days."

"Mrs. Meadows, three days for somebody in the entertainment business is not all that long."

"It is when you're having an affair with them."

I didn't know what to say to that, so I let it slide.

"Mr. Baca, I've talked to him several times a day, every day for the last two months."

"You still haven't told me why you think he's missing."

"I believe my husband found out about us."

"Did your husband confront you?"

"No. Look, Mr. Baca, I'm willing to pay you, so is there some sort of problem?"

"I'm not against making money, Mrs. Meadows, but I don't take advantage of clients, either."

"Mrs. Meadows sounds so old. Call me Bond, and don't worry about taking advantage of me. I can take care of myself. When can you start?"

"Don't you want to discuss fees?"

"You don't seem like the type to haggle. I'll give you five thousand dollars up front and you can bill me as you like if you need more."

I didn't let her see me swallow. "You're not worried I'll drag this out?"

"I talked to several people in the business about you, Mr. Baca-"

"Call me Ronny. Mr. Baca sounds so old."

She gave me a small smile, "-and they assured me you don't work that way. Matt and Ben said you might come across as a wise-ass, but you were honest and your work was good."

I said, "Matt and Ben?"

"They said you helped one of their friends. Others who are outside the entertainment industry said you get things done."

"Nice to have your own fan club."

"Oh, they aren't fans." She stood up, removed a large stack of hundreds, counted out fifty of them and placed the money on my desk along with a business card and a sheet of paper with information printed on it. "I don't need a receipt. The paper has information on Bob you might find useful. If you need me, call the number on the card. It's my business cell phone. I always have it with me. Thank you." She walked out, closing the door behind her.

I looked at the money. Okay, I thought. How hard can it be to find a famous Hollywood movie star? It's not as if people won't recognize him. The guy had been on more magazine covers in the last year than the Olsen twins had in their entire lives. I looked at the typed paper and found Landman's address in Pacific Palisades, license plates and descriptions for vehicles, an address on a Malibu home, his personal assistant's phone number and the phone number and location of Landman's office on the lot at Americas Studios. There were about ten cell phone numbers, all shown as Bob's, and a description of a customized yellow Colnago Oval Master mountain bike he owned. I wondered if I should call Bond and tell her she'd left off his zodiac sign and biorhythm chart.

I got up from the chair and went into the bathroom to shower and change. No sense in greeting the next clients barefooted and in gym shorts.

I slipped on a dark blue short-sleeved shirt, gray pleated pants and matching gray New Balance tennis shoes. The shoulder holster with my Model 19 Smith and Wesson went on like a lover's embrace and I covered it with a new, gunmetal gray Patagonia windbreaker I had practically stolen. I looked at my reflection in the mirror. Good enough for the cover of GQ...or Guns and Ammo.

I opened the bathroom door and saw my partner, Hondo Wells sitting on the corner of my desk, looking at the scattered hundreds covering the top.

"Hey, I had that in my drawer."

"I smelled it when I came in."

"You *smelled* it? Well shoot, let's take you up north and look for D.B. Cooper's money."

Hondo said, "So you've got forty-two hundred dollars here-"

"Hey, there's five thousand."

"Gotcha. What are we being paid to investigate?"

I filled him in as he restacked the money and put a rubber band around it.

Hondo said, "We'll take my car."

"What's wrong with mine?"

"I'm not going through that neighborhood in Shamu." Hondo insisted we take his vehicle since he'd washed it and it would blend in better than my pickup, which is a two-year old four-wheel-drive Ford 250 pickup with oversized tires and front and rear bumpers made of welded six-inch iron pipe painted black. The windows are tinted black and the pickup is painted black except for white teardrop shapes along the headlights and white along the bottom third of the side panels and doors. That's why Hondo calls it Shamu. I'd taken it as payment on a case and he hasn't let me live it down. Hondo on the other hand drives a prissy looking gold Mercedes convertible. He denies its prissy looking, but it is.

We'd used a *Map To The Stars' Homes* in a case last year and I had it with me as we drove through Pacific Palisades. I pointed ahead, "Look, that's Arnold's old house."

Hondo used one finger to pull the Ray Bans down on his nose and look at me.

"Hey, I like his movies." Landman's residence was several houses further down, and Hondo eased by the driveway and iron gate, stopping just beyond. I walked back and looked through the bars.

The house was a combination of Spanish Mediterranean and Early Love Boat. A red tile roof above white stucco walls three stories high made up a house that must have contained forty thousand square feet. Round windows the size of whiskey barrels ran in regular intervals around each story like portholes, and the arched double front doors were massive white marble slabs inscribed with black lines and runes. Each door was about ten feet high and five feet wide, looking like something you would open to enter The Mines of Moria.

A Lincoln sat in the circular drive and as I watched, one of the home's massive doors swung open and a slender woman with blond, spiky hair, wearing a lime green blouse and Capri pants the color of walnuts walked around the car and stopped at the driver's door. On a hunch I pulled Bond's folded paper out of my jacket, located the number for Landman's personal assistant and dialed it on my cell. As it rang in my ear, I watched the slender woman reach into her purse. She pulled out a cell phone and put it to her ear.

    I heard, "Hello?"

    "Miss Haile, Mickey Haile?"

    "Yes, who is this?"

    "My name is Ronald Baca. I'm a private investigator who's been hired by someone close to Mr. Landman." Mickey Haile moved around, taking two or three little steps, then turning and doing it again, like a windup toy soldier that bumps into things and only goes a few steps before changing direction.

    "What? What do you want?"

    "I want to locate Robert Landman."

    More turning, walking, turning, and a little hair tugging. "I don't...I can relay your message to Mr. Landman. If you'd like to leave your number..."

    "Can I come by and give it to you personally?"

    "Yes, yes, sure-"

    "You're sure it's okay to give it to you person-to-person?"

    More hair tugging, "Yes! You can come by the off-"

    "How about right now? I'm at the gate." She looked at the gate and I waved a big, side-to-side Howdy-Do at her. From her reaction, it was a good thing she was wearing brown slacks.

**

After Mickey opened the gate, Hondo parked the Mercedes by the Lincoln and we walked to the marble doors where she held one side open. Hondo left on his sunglasses, going for the mysterious effect.

    Mickey was a nervous wreck, with shaking, jerky hands and dark circles under her eyes that makeup didn't quite cover. Her short hair looked like it had been savaged by an attacking squirrel, and I could smell that she hadn't bathed in several days.

    Hondo can't stand bad smells, and I was surprised he didn't run onto the lawn and rub his face in the grass like a skunk-sprayed dog. Instead, he smiled and walked beside her into an enormous den with floor to ceiling bookcases, a huge black marble fireplace that could hold a small tree, several comfortable chairs and one desk with a black marble top as big as a sheet of plywood.

One thing about Bob Landman, he kept the marble industry healthy. The odd thing about the bookcases was the absence of books. There was room for five thousand volumes, and nothing was there but empty space.

Mickey sat in a chair near the unlit fireplace. Well, sat isn't the right word. She *perched*, maybe an inch of her rear on the front edge of the seat cushion, with her back ramrod straight and her hands picking and pulling at each other as her eyes darted from me to Hondo and back again.

Hondo sat on the sofa across from her and said, "Its okay, Mickey. We're worried about him, too."

It was as if the sprinkler system came on. Mickey buh-hawed and more tears came than I'd imagined could come from two eyes. Big drops one right after the other, building and dropping from her lashes and off her nose and chin and plopping on the floor like marble-sized rain.

Hondo looked at me and motioned with his head toward her. I walked over to Mickey and placed a hand on her thin shoulder. "Mickey, it's okay. We just want to find him, make sure he's all right. Make sure he's not in any trouble." That started another round of hawing and head shaking.

"There, there," I said and patted her shoulder. Suddenly Mickey stood up and hugged me close with a surprising spidery strength, crying her eyes out on my gray windbreaker, smearing mascara, snot, and tears all over the front where she rubbed her face back and forth. I held her until the crying subsided to sobs and shudders and gasps, and then to whimpers and small keenings and finally to deep, exhausted breathing.

She raised her face to look up at me. Gene Simmons in his Kiss days had less black around the eyes. She gave me the same look a shooting victim gives the first paramedic to reach them. "C-Can you find him? Oh, please?"

"We think what you can tell us might get us closer."

"I don't know anything. Bob, he...he was at the office Wednesday and said he'd see me the next day, and then...he disappeared."

I sat her down and took a vacant chair. "How did you try to reach him? When did you first miss him? Take us through every step."

Mickey attempted to push down the spikes of hair as she thought it through, "It was the next morning after he missed two studio meetings, nine and ten o'clock. I tried his car phone - the one in his Ferrari, not the Hummer - I tried that later, then I called his home, his personal cell phone, his office cell phone and the studio cell phone. I tried the studio, the home in Malibu, his yacht in Marina Del Rey, and I left e-mails on all five of his computers and those of Mr. Meadows' executive assistant. I've done that every day since he's been gone."

I looked at Hondo, but couldn't read anything behind the sunglasses. Hondo said, "You call any people he hangs out with?"

"Yes, all one hundred and twenty four names I have in my rolodex."

Hondo cocked his head, "Are there any people you might not have listed? New acquaintances, someone special?"

Mickey acted offended. "No, I know everyone Mr. Landman considers phoneable."

Phoneable? This girl would be a riot at a scrabble tournament. I said, "Mickey, pest control is *phoneable*. Couldn't there be someone you don't have listed?"

She gnawed at the skin around her thumbnail as she thought. After two minutes, I worried that her teeth might scrape bone, but she finally spoke. "He did make some calls from his office. They were funny."

"Funny ha-ha or funny weird?"

"Funny weird. He would close the door and use a cell phone. I noticed because the line wouldn't light up on my phone."

Hondo asked, "Did he make a call like that on Wednesday?"

Mickey chewed another inch of skin from her thumb before saying, "Yes. He called about four in the afternoon, and he left a half hour later."

I asked, "Are you sure of the time?"

"Yes, because the Fed-Ex man came and I signed for a package at three fifty-five and it was right after that. And he left at four-thirty because I had to cancel a four forty-five meeting for him."

Hondo looked at me, "We can find out who he called pretty easy that way. Might be something."

"We'll check it out." Mickey began wringing her hands and her eyes filled. I said, "Mickey, we're going to find him. You've been a big help."

Mickey started bawling again, and after she grabbed me and buried her face on my chest, I wondered if my nipples would prune from all the moisture.

**

After Mickey dried out we had her write down any of Landman's phone numbers we didn't have, the name and location of his yacht, and then we walked around the house to see which vehicles were and weren't there. He had fourteen, and all were there, even the Hummer, painted with scenes that were god-awful.

Mickey said, "Bob was feeling very Southwestern when he had it painted. He hired Valdar, you know, the Volga artist? He's staying at Bob's Malibu house for a few months while he gathers the essence of the American experience."

Saguaro cactus, buttes, and howling coyotes that looked more like Lassie than wild canines silhouetted against a full moon. The worst image in the scene was of a party of six Fabio-looking Indian warriors – four of them blondes – on horseback dressed in Plains Indian costumes including braids and full headdresses with feathered tails flowing in some unseen breeze. You'd think Valdar could have gotten the right Indian Nation for the terrain. Mickey continued, "It's very masculine, don't you think?" She was practically wetting her pants.

To keep from getting soaked I said, "It's ah...unique." Hondo was in the corner of my vision and I saw him shake his head in slow motion.

We'd left then, but not before Mickey gave me a hug and big kiss on the cheek, her private cell phone number, her home phone number, office and home e-mail, and her address. Hondo asked her if the Lincoln was her only vehicle and she said no, she also had a Volkswagen Bug, one of the new ones, and oh, Bob had had his artist paint it with tiny cactus and coyotes, too, so they would match. She squirmed as she talked, like she had to go to the bathroom. "Bob had Valdar paint Indian maidens instead of the warriors. Wasn't that just the most thoughtful, darling thing?"

We got the license number to go with the description of the paint job.

As we left Mickey and drove out the gate I said, "Looks like she's in love with her boss."

Hondo nodded, "Yep."

"So, Landman was having an affair with Bond *and* Mickey."

"This is LA," Hondo said, "Happens all the time. But maybe it's just infatuation on Mickey's part. Maybe there's nothing going on."

"She does lean toward melodrama, I noticed that."

"Did you notice the other thing?"

"What other thing?"

"Mickey is a man."

CHAPTER TWO

I looked at him.

Hondo held his thumb against his throat and made a half-inch space between it and his forefinger. "Adam's apple."

I was silent for a moment before saying, "I didn't catch that."

Hondo glanced at me as he turned on Sunset. "I figured all you could see was the top of her hair. Between that and worrying about all that mascara getting on your windbreaker, you were a little preoccupied. By the way, your jacket looks like one of those tee-shirts that kids wore years ago, the ones that had big black and red splotches on them and below that it said 'I ran into Tammye Faye at the mall', you remember."

I tried to clean the windbreaker with my handkerchief, but it only smeared. I gave up and said, "At least Mickey seemed capable, and with the cell numbers it'll be easy to check since we know the time and date of the call."

"Mucho simple since all those phones are with the same company."

"He does their commercials and gets them for free."

Hondo slipped around a red Ferrari and got us to the office in record time.

∗∗

It was an hour before my friend at the Sheriff's office called back. He said there was no record of any of the phone numbers I'd given him making a call at that time. I hung up and looked at Hondo, who was sharpening his Black Ops folding knife, the same one he'd carried when we were in Afghanistan.

"No record of any calls."

Hondo tested the blade by running it across his forearm. Hair rolled up like a military barber working the heads of new recruits. He folded it and put it in his pocket. "We need to double check the office phone. Maybe for some reason, Mickey's light to that line didn't work."

"Yeah or maybe she's lying."

"Or maybe Bob was arguing with ghosts."

I got back on the phone and said to Hondo while I re-dialed my friend at the Sheriff's office, "Let's check the office phone first, see if he used it. If that doesn't work, then we'll call a medium."

"And if that doesn't work, we need to go back to square one."

I nodded as I asked my friend for another favor and Hondo grinned as he heard the tinny yell come out of the receiver and into my ear.

**

After getting nowhere again, Hondo said he was hungry for Moroccan, so we left the office and drove in my truck to *Tagine* on Robertson Boulevard. It's in Beverly Hills, and as usual, we got a few stares at Shamu. We finished lunch and Hondo was working on dessert when he said, "We can check the credit cards, see if there's been any activity."

"Yeah, maybe check the bank for ATM withdrawals or checks written."

"I can do those. You going to check with the Meadows woman again?"

"I think so." I thought for a moment, "There's something about her I can't quite place. I've seen her somewhere before, or heard her name, but can't pin it down."

Hondo chewed, swallowed and said, "Was her maiden name Savitch?"

It clicked. Bond Savitch. That was her, all right. Maybe five, six years ago. She had been a blond then, and wore dark sunglasses everywhere except the courtroom. The trial lasted six months, with extensive coverage a la OJ. In the end, she was found not guilty in the killing of her lover, but the public perception was not as clear-cut. There were vague circumstances and evidence not adequately explained, forensics experts spoke with eloquence for both sides, and the jury deliberated two days before reaching the verdict. Many people thought she got off with murder, but being LA and the fact that she was so beautiful, others said, "What do you expect?"

I hadn't followed the case and didn't know how he'd died, but with courtroom scenes on the news every hour of the day, it was impossible not to know of the trial.

I said, "So, that's her."

"I think so." Hondo said. "Be aware of that, uh? She killed him with a bottle of Cristal."

"She forced him to drink a bottle of champagne and it killed him?"

He stopped chewing and looked at me.

"Nooo. She hit him with it. Knocked him down and shattered the bottle. While he was on his hands and knees, she jabbed the broken half at the side of his face and cut his jugular. Guy bled to death in about ten seconds."

He took another bite, then pointed with his chin to indicate something over my shoulder. "You're going to have to move Shamu again."

I turned to look and Ryan Gosling walked into the restaurant, smiling and talking to everyone but looking around.

"Oops," I said.

"I told you not to park in his space."

"It's not like there aren't other places he can park, jeez."

"He's one of the owners."

Gosling spotted us and put his hands on his hips. I waved at him and he didn't smile, just jerked his head to the side. I can read head-language, so I said to Hondo, "I'll just go move the truck, be waiting for you outside."

Hondo grinned as he forked up the last bites. "Oh yeah."

**

I ran some errands in Hollywood and called Bond's cell phone from the truck. She said she would be waiting for me at home. I asked which home and after a second's silence, she said the one in Beverly.

Driving from Hollywood into Beverly Hills is the American statement to everyone where the line between the haves and have-nots begins. On the one side are shops, small homes, old cars, lots of pickups and lowriders, Mexicans, blacks, derelicts and winos, with a smattering of tourists and gawkers, out of work actors. Lots of unkempt lawns are around, as are children and young people.

The moment you cross into Beverly Hills, it's like black and white Dorothy opening the door and seeing Technicolor Oz. Emerald green lawns and hedges manicured and worried to perfection, large trees and exquisite landscapes showcasing huge, beautiful homes that cost more than a thousand of the have-nots combined would make in a hundred years.

There were no old cars, no trash, no dusty streets, and only occasional glimpses of children. It was stunning and remote, an urban Eden, showing the drive by gawkers with every passing block how far apart their worlds were from those who lived behind the ornate doors and gates.

As I pulled up to the Meadows' gate and punched in the numbers Bond had written down, a five-year old station wagon with Oklahoma plates and what must have been a husband and wife and forty kids, judging from all the arms and legs I saw sticking out of the windows, slowed to a stop and stared at me open-mouthed.

I guess I have that celebrity look. As the gate opened, I waved at them and started my pickup forward. One of the kids yelled something that I couldn't make out, so I stopped and put my head out the window so they could go back and tell their neighbors they visited with a famous star at his home.

"You the gardener?"

"What?" I said.

"Are you the gardener? Which star lives here?"

"What makes you think I'm not the star?"

The kid, maybe fifteen and wearing a red Sooners ball cap, took a long look at my black pickup and said, "We figured, with that truck..."

"What's wrong with my truck?"

There was some conversation in the station wagon I couldn't hear, and the wagon started to pull away. The kid in the Sooners cap stuck his head out of the window and said, "Your truck looks like that fish at Sea World!"

"It's not a fish, it's a mammal!"

The station wagon drove out of sight and I went through the gate. Tourists.

Bond opened the door and let me in. She was wearing a white Turkish robe and her hair was wet. The inside of the house was spacious, elegant, with a winding stairway leading to the second floor. I followed her through the house for what seemed like the length of a football field before we emerged in the back yard beside an Olympic-sized pool complete with ten-meter diving platform. Surrounding the pool and lounge area was a manicured garden that went all the way to the rock wall surrounding the three-acre yard.

Huge topiary figures shaped from the shrubs and bushes bordered the pool area. The closest ones were of a rhino that was ten feet high, rearing on its hind legs like a stallion, and a twelve-foot high kangaroo with a joey's head sticking out of the pouch.

Completing the lineup were elephants, lions, bears, a pod of three porpoises surfing on green leafy waves, and what looked like a cross between a ten-foot vulture and a smiling pterodactyl. Creepy things like these had haunted my childhood dreams and I kept picking them up from of the corner of my eye as if they had moved.

Bond led us to a shaded table and we sat in patio chairs that were more comfortable than anything I had in my apartment, including the bed. There was a magnum of champagne iced in a bucket and two glasses on the table beside us. It was Cristal.

Bond shook her wet hair and the drops caught the sun like sparkling lights. The white Turkish bathrobe had somehow come undone during our walk and revealed large glimpses of tanned, taut skin and rounded breasts.

Bond asked, "Would you like some champagne?"

"No thank you." She poured herself a glass and I watched to make sure she didn't flip the bottle and grab it by the neck. As she poured, the robe opened like a coin purse, revealing a tight, perfect stomach as golden as the rest of her. I felt the urge to flex but held off. I didn't want her to swoon before we talked.

"We talked to Mickey at Landman's home. She seems stressed about his disappearance. I was wondering, did you tell her not to notify the police?"

"Yes. We talked it over and both agreed it would serve nothing at this point."

"Okay, at what point do you think it would serve something?"

She sat up, "You can get that tone out of your voice. Mickey and I made the decision together and I felt that hiring you would be the best thing to do. It seemed a hell of a lot better than calling the police before we even know if anything's wrong. What's the matter, aren't I paying you enough?" She shifted and a lot more sleek skin showed.

"The pay's fine. Looking at your body is very fine. But there may come a time when the police will need to be notified. You understand?"

She said, "My, aren't you forceful?"

If she knew how strong her pheromones were affecting me, she wouldn't have mentioned forceful. I was ready to bellow and attack matadors with my horns. But I controlled it and said, "Look, you hired me to find him, and I will. But if I discover things that make me worry about his well being, I will contact the police."

"Without me authorizing it?" She leaned forward as if to make a point and her breasts pushed further out of the robe, revealing two brown crescents.

I reached forward and pulled her robe together. "Keep it that way while we talk."

She sat back, and then tied the robe together. Her eyes held a look I couldn't make out.

I said, "You're a beautiful woman, but this is business. If I feel Landman's in danger, I won't wait for you to tell me to wag my tail or to fetch. There's no negotiation on this."

We sat there for several minutes. She looked at the water in the pool for most of the time, then watched me before saying, "I can live with that. You'll keep me informed of everything you find out. Agreed?"

"Agreed." With most of her body covered, my pulse slowed down. My heart had been banging so hard I was worried about my pocket pen springing a leak. I asked, "Where's your husband? I'll need to talk to him."

"He's at his office on the lot." She bit at her lip after she spoke.

I nodded. "I'll try and catch him there. I won't say who hired me."

"If he's not at Americas, you might try Siberia on the Sunset Strip. He's there a great deal lately. Usually with his personal assistant, Carl Rakes."

"What about this Rakes?"

"He's a Russian that Frank met about three years ago. Frank hired Carl and doesn't go anywhere without him."

I got up and said, "I'll keep in touch."

**

Hondo called me on my cell as I drove down Sunset. He said, "I struck out on this end. You do any good?"

"Nope. Frank wasn't at the studio, so I'm headed to some place called Siberia on Sunset to talk to him, see if I can dig up anything that way."

"Try the Tunguska Blast while you're there."

"The what?"

"The Tunguska Blast, named after the comet that hit Tunguska."

"I know about the comet, what's the drink?"

"They make it with vodka that's chilled to somewhere around minus twenty degrees Fahrenheit and mixed with some kind of mint and their special secret ingredients that are imported from the Tunguska area in Siberia, and something else that I think is Sprite, then they shoot compressed pure oxygen into it until it foams, and then you drink it."

"And you want me to try that?"

"Sure. It's not like anything else you've ever tasted. They say the oxygen aeration also keeps you from having a hangover."

I thought about asking him how swallowing bubbles of oxygenated vodka into my stomach would keep me from a hangover since the oxygen wouldn't be in my lungs, but wasn't sure I was ready for his explanation.

Hondo said, "Well, I've got something else I want to check. I'll go back to the house and do a little looking."

I knew he meant Landman's mansion. "Do you have a key?"

"Oh sure, I can get in. Later."

I put away the cell phone and rubbed my forehead. With Hondo, sometimes it is best not to ask.

**

Siberia was located in one of those buildings on the Sunset Strip that have had a hundred different club names since the sixties. I parked and got out of my truck to look it over and watch people going in. Siberia looked like a place for the rougher element and not the usual choice of entertainment executives, although I recognized some of the younger acting crowd going inside. I went in and let my eyes adjust.

The decor was something out of a B movie. The walls were covered from floor to ceiling with blow-ups of photographs of the actual Tunguska blast site. It showed a forest of conifer trees blown flat, stripped of branches, and extending as far as the eye could see over the rises in the distance. Complete devastation, with the trunks laid out like thousands of dominoes knocked flat. The photos had been color tinted and looked as good as Ted Turner's techniques on old black and white movies.

Half of the tables and chair backs were made of pine logs laid out to flow in the same direction as the wall photographs of felled trees. I guess that was to give the customer a feel of being in the center of the blast. There was another area consisting of sofas, love seats and armchairs that commanded the space between the dance floor and the pool tables.

The bar was thirty feet long, with comfortable looking stools and a brass foot-rail. Behind it in the corner was a two-tiered table with a large barrel the size of a whiskey keg on top. Below it were racks of what must have been a dozen silver cylinders that looked like quarter-sized aqua-lungs, complete with regulators and small black tubes running from them. The tanks had shoulder straps and it looked like the cylinders would ride high, not reaching lower than mid back. As I watched, a cute waitress went to the stack, got one and put it on. She checked the nozzle and I heard it hiss. Must be the compressed oxygen Hondo mentioned.

Siberia was doing pretty good for an afternoon crowd. Eight guys in leather jackets with cut-off sleeves were in the corner shooting pool, and another twenty or thirty people were arranged around the room and standing at the bar. The young acting crowd was standing together on the dance floor, deciding where to sit. The smell of cigarette smoke was faint, and I could hear multiple exhaust fans working overtime to keep the air clean. They were powerful, too. I walked under one and felt the upward breeze ruffle my hair. The Red Hot Chili Peppers played on the sound system, but not loud enough to make the patrons yell to be heard by each other. The ratio was five to one men-to-women, but a couple of the women looked like they could hold their own.

A young waitress dressed in silver hot pants and matching sports bra and wearing one of the silver aqua lungs stopped and asked what I'd like. Might as well be reckless, I thought. "I'll have a Tunguska Blast."

She smiled, "Very good, sir." and left. I watched her walk away and thought the silver aqua-lung thingee went well with the view of her rounded silver behind.

I spotted Frank Meadows sitting on one of the love seats, talking to a massive black bodybuilder. The bodybuilder was shirtless; wearing suspenders with his Levi's and work boots. Five feet behind Frank was a big, rawboned man leaning against the wall. I took this to be Carl Rakes. His hair was long and dirty-blond, hanging to his shoulders. He wore a white, long-sleeved shirt and jeans. He had his thumbs hooked in the jeans pockets. I could make out the dark edges of tattoos peeking beyond the cuffs.

The waitress came back with my drink and balanced it on the tray while she fished a pencil-thin black hose from over her shoulder and shot a noisy blast of air into the tall drink. It bubbled and fizzed and, I swear, changed colors as I watched.

"Cheers," she said. "It's best to knock it back all at once." I took the drink from the tray and she smiled again, "That'll be twenty dollars, or shall I run a tab?"

"Twenty dollars?"

"Yes sir. The cost of importing the Tunguska's secret ingredients are very expensive. They are unique in the world."

I paid her and tipped five more for the privilege of watching her walk away again. Oh well. I looked at the drink and it had stopped fizzing. I tossed it back.

It went down like molten heat and made a silent explosion in my stomach, then spread like the blast of an A-bomb. It was a cold-hot thing, like menthol, but not severe. I felt it running through my veins all the way to my fingers and toes and up to my head.

Roto-Rooter couldn't have opened my sinus cavities any wider and it felt like every capillary in my lungs was drawing a super charge of oxygen and shooting it through my system. My eyes watered a little as I breathed. Good grief, this stuff was so good it was probably illegal in seven states. I came back to normal and thought about ordering another one, but decided to pass for now.

I walked toward Frank but watched Rakes. He appeared to be almost asleep. If you looked a little closer, you could see he was alert, aware of everything around the room, including me as I approached Meadows.

Carl came off the wall as smooth as magic and stepped in front of me. He said, "Thad is far enough. I help you?"

He was bigger than I thought, one of those well-proportioned people who look average until you are beside them.

This guy was a good five inches taller than me. He had some major halitosis, too. I said, "You bet you can. There's some mouthwash for sale across the street. You go buy yourself a quart, gargle that around awhile so we can start healing the ozone layer. Hey, better yet buy yourself one of those Tunguska Blasts. That'll clean your tonsils."

Frank and the bodybuilder stopped talking to watch us.

Frank said, "Can't. He's allergic."

"Allergic?"

"He drinks one, his eyes water and he starts coughing, nose stops up, all that stuff."

I looked at Rakes and said, "Choke up over your Mother country, huh? Well, that still leaves the mouthwash across the street."

Carl said, "You come oudside for me, ve talk inside my breath." He started to put his hand on me and I slapped it away. He grinned. "Oh, I vill like dis."

The back of a black sofa was behind him so I gave him a sharp push -- his body felt hard, like someone made of gristle and bone -- and his legs caught on the edge and he went over, but not like I'd planned.

In a twisting acrobatic move amazing for someone his size, Carl turned in the air as he was falling and did a somersault, landing on the balls of his feet on the opposite side of the sofa, facing me. "You peckershid, I ged you now," he said.

Peckershid? I said, "Russian Ebonics don't impress me, Igor. I'm here about Bob Landman, and I need to talk to Frank Meadows, not waltz with you in the parking lot."

Meadows looked at me, "I know you?"

"No, you don't. I've been hired to locate Bob Landman, and I need to ask you a few questions."

"You private?" I nodded.

"What's your name?"

"Ronny Baca."

"Baca, huh? You don't look like a spic."

"My parents were from Bolognia. It's a province in France."

Meadows nodded his head like he'd heard of the place, then said to Rakes, "It's okay." Carl went back to his place against the wall as if nothing had happened.

Meadows asked, "So, what's this about Bob?"

"He hasn't been heard from in three days. Some people close to him are worried. I'm trying to locate him."

The bodybuilder started to leave and Frank said, "You bulk up a little more, you know what I mean, then we'll talk about you being the next Scorpion King." The bodybuilder had biceps over twenty inches. The only thing left for him was steroids or an increase in steroids if he was already on them, which he probably was. "Now go," Frank said. The bodybuilder left and Frank turned to me, "Okay, some people are worried about Bobby Landman, some people close to him. What do they expect me to do? I'm not his nursemaid. He's a grown man, rich, he can go anywhere. He's done this before, leaving for several weeks and coming back to tell everybody how he got in touch with himself. What crap." Frank motioned for me to sit down and said, "What can I tell you. I haven't talked to Bobby in about a week, since he came to the office to do his latest pitch. Where he is and what he's doing, I don't know."

"Do you socialize much with him?"

"You mean go to parties? Sure, my wife and I have been to lots of parties with Landman. Last one was two, three months ago. Can't see how that would help you."

If this guy knew his wife was fooling around with Robert Landman, well, he could play a great hand of poker. I gave him my card and said, "If you hear from him, would you contact me at that number? I would appreciate it."

He smiled at me and tore the card, dropping the pieces on the floor. He said, "You've got all the time you'll ever get with me. Leave, or I'll let Carl have you." Carl came off the wall and started toward me. I stood and thought about drawing my magnum, but wasn't sure six rounds would be enough to stop the advancing Cro-Magnon.

There was a movement in the darkness behind Carl and I saw Hondo reach him. Carl came to a stop like a charging dog hitting the end of a chain. I couldn't tell how Hondo was holding him, but Carl only struggled a little before shrugging his shoulders and stopping. Hondo made a quarter turn with Carl so he could see Frank and me. No one in the place was paying any attention.

Hondo said, "Figured I'd better stop old Too-Tall here before you did him some serious harm."

Frank snorted and said, "Let him go. Carl, don't worry about these two." Hondo released his grip and Carl turned to look him up and down. He gave Hondo a slight nod and went to his wall. Hondo stood where he was, smiling and looking all mellow.

I turned my attention to Meadows. "We're not looking for a pissing contest, Frank," his eyebrows went up at the use of his first name, "We're trying to locate someone who should be valuable to you. I'm having a hard time deciding why you don't want that to happen."

"You start messing with me, you're going to get your balls handed to you on a plate."

I rolled my eyes, "Frank, listen to me. I'm not messing with you. I'm going to find Bob Landman. Your cooperation might have made it easier, but we don't need you to do this."

He smiled and exhaled, "Maybe you're right." He took a step closer with his hand out as if to shake, but when I relaxed, Frank hopped to within an inch of me and shot his hand to my crotch. He was a powerful man, with forearms like a blacksmith and his grip on me took my breath away. His face was an inch from mine as he said, "Your cojones on a plate, you fuck with me." He let go and stepped back, watching my reaction. Carl was still against the wall, and Hondo hadn't moved.

I didn't move either, partly because the pain was almost paralyzing me, but also because I was not going to let him see he'd gotten to me.

I crossed my arms on my chest, cocked one leg, and kept a blank face as I almost screamed like a girl when my scrotum adjusted. "You want to grab men like that, you better go to a gay bar and get a date. It doesn't impress me." I turned and walked toward the door. Hondo watched the two of them until I drew even. Carl pointed his hand at us with the thumb cocked and forefinger extended and mouthed "Bang," as we walked out the door.

As soon as the door closed behind us, I sucked in a large breath of air, leaned against the wall and fought against throwing up.

"Good thing that didn't hurt, huh?" Hondo said.

I stood up and walked toward my truck, taking small, slow steps that gradually increased in length as the ache left my stomach and settled low in the groin, like my pelvic bones were cradling a shovel full of hot coals. Hondo opened the door for me and I took two tries before making it into the seat. I unbuttoned and unzipped my pants before buckling on the seatbelt.

Hondo said, "Go on home. I'll see you in the morning."

As he turned to leave I asked, "Did you find anything at the house?"

"Yeah. Landman's mountain bike was missing. That's a three thousand dollar bike. You don't just misplace one of those."

I thought about that as I readjusted my position in the seat, all the while using my hands to cradle my swelling gonads.

Powder monkey's didn't hold jars of nitro with any more care than I was holding my balls.

Hondo closed the driver's door for me and said, "I'd put some ice on those tonight or you're going to have the Lakers wanting to borrow them to shoot hoops." He left as I started Shamu. My trip home was done at a blazing speed of forty miles an hour, and despite the pain, all I could think of was Bob Landman and his mountain bike.

**

The next morning Hondo came by and picked me up. As I walked to the Mercedes and got in he said, "Looks like you're holding a cheeseburger between your legs when you walk."

"Drive," I said. He grinned and maneuvered us down Mulholland Drive, in and out of traffic as smooth as a skier in deep powder. We turned on Ventura, then took the Pacific Coast Highway all the way into Venice. The day was beautiful, with no haze in the air, everything in crisp focus, and the smell of the sea perfumed the morning.

We parked in the gym's lot, which was already three-quarters full and went to the office. We sat in our chairs and talked things through. There was no real indication that Bob Landman had met with foul play, but Frank Meadows didn't seem to care that Landman wasn't around. Could be because his wife was playing choo-choo with the actor, but if it was, Frank could keep it hidden on his face. If not, then maybe Meadows was right, and Landman had gone off to find himself.

That left Bond...and Mickey. Both of them close to the actor, seeing and talking to him every day and suddenly, *poof*, he's Twilight Zoned out of here without either one of them having a clue about it. That's the part that bothered us. Hondo took the paper with Mickey's number and while he dialed, I went into the storage room where I kept some clothes and changed into looser fitting pants. I left off the Haines, too.

Hondo hung up the phone as I walked back to my desk. He said, "You borrow those from MC Hammer?"

I sat down, "These are called relaxed-fit jeans. The latest thing."

"Uh-huh," Hondo grinned, then said, "Mickey said Landman used to ride his bike a lot on the trails into the Santa Monica Mountains. She said there's one trail several blocks behind his house that was his favorite."

"We should head up that way, then. Check it out."

"It wouldn't take much to fall into one of those canyons and not be found for a while. It's rugged up there in places."

"We'd better get some gear, a couple of bikes-"

Hondo held up his hand, "You don't have to worry. It's all taken care of."

"When did you do that?"

"Oh, I didn't. Mickey did. She got three bikes, said she'd meet us at the start of the trail."

Oh great.

CHAPTER THREE

We changed into shorts and tee shirts and we both wore our New Balance trail shoes. I left my pistol at the office, but Hondo put his Glock forty-five under the driver's seat of the Mercedes. The Black Ops knife he put in his short pocket.

As we rounded the last curve to the trail, we saw the parked BMW and Mickey standing nearby in the shade of a small tree, with three bikes lined up like soldiers beside her. Mickey waved and jumped up and down when she saw us, as excited as a kid. She didn't have to wave. No one was going to miss her in the hot pink and lime-green spandex biking shorts and matching spandex top she was wearing. She wore a small purple fanny pack, and her hair was a spiky, punked mohawk that had green and pink glitter gelled into it.

Hondo said, "Man, even her shoes are pink." He was right. So was her bike, at least I assumed it was hers. She hurried over to the car as we stopped.

"I am sooo glad to see you two again. It gives me such a sense of security with two big macho guys on the case. I just know we'll make a great team." She almost squealed with the last words.

"Ahh, Mickey --"

"You're right Mickey," Hondo said, "That's exactly what Ronny told me on the way here."

Mickey blushed. I swear. She looked at me and said, "Thank you, Ronny. Most people don't like me around. They uh, well...I don't hear very many nice things come my way. It was nice, what you said."

I felt like an ass.

Hondo said, "Which bike is mine?"

Mickey clapped her hands in delight, then took one of ours in each of hers and led us to them. "Yours, Hondo, is the black one, and Ronny's is the white one. Mine's the pink one." *Thank goodness.* They were Colnagos, expensive bikes.

"Where'd you get these?"

"The dealer keeps them at his shop. They're Bob's."

"How many does he have?"

"Twelve, well thirteen counting mine. Bob did a commercial in France for Colnago and part of his contract called for receipt of them as an incentive. He just wanted to have a different one for each month."

"He changes bikes each month?"

"Well, he did until the yellow one became his favorite. After he was photographed on it for the cover of People Magazine, he felt it matched his hair better."

His hair. What a reason to pick a three thousand dollar bicycle. "And that's the bike he had at the house."

"Yes. It's the only one he's ridden in the last six months."

Hondo adjusted his seat and was ready to go. Mickey hopped on her bike and moved it from the shade into the sun. The light on all that bright pink and green made my eyes squint, like looking at a neon sign from three inches away.

Mickey led out, saying over her shoulder, "I rode with Bob many times on this trail. He had two favorite routes that I thought we could try first." Mickey may have really been a male and only about five-six and one-twenty, but that pink bike was *moving*. By the time I adjusted my seat and was pedaling, they were already two hundred yards ahead. I stood up and leaned into it, changing gears and moving my feet fast on the pedals so that in ten minutes I pulled up beside Hondo. I readjusted myself several times on the seat and couldn't find a comfortable position.

Hondo said, "I bet riding that tiny seat hurts something fierce."

"No worse than hopping on a running chainsaw." I wiggled again and found a position that was a little better.

Hondo said, "Yeah, but that squeeze old Frank gave you would have killed a lesser man." He grinned at me, then sped up beside Mickey and told her to watch the right side, that he would watch the left and I would watch both.

We had the trail to ourselves so far, and the sun on us felt warm and penetrating. I had a good sweat going. My muscles limbered up and the pain between my legs lessened to that of a throbbing bad tooth. There hadn't been much rain and the brush on the hillsides and in the canyons had a brown, brittle look, making what green shrubs and trees there were stand out like fresh paint. Dust stayed in the air behind us as we moved higher, following the contours of the ridges in a steady upward angle.

Two hours later, we reached the main fork. Mickey moved under the shade and we followed her. Her cheeks were flushed and her eyes bright with energy. "Wow, that is *sooo* exhilarating." There was fine sweat on Mickey's face, but she must have been wearing waterproof mascara today because it hadn't run. Hondo and I were huffing and I could feel the tremble in my thighs from that last climb.

Hondo said, "What's down that one?" He pointed to the left fork.

Mickey said, "That's Bob's long trail. It winds across and west, then back. It's about two hours."

"More?" I said.

"Yes, silly. It's the long route." She pointed to the right hand path, "That's the short one. It only takes an hour."

"More?"

Mickey waved her finger at me. "You just want to make me feel good. An athletic looking man like you could ride all day. I appreciate it, but you don't have to hold back on my account."

Hondo said, "Yeah, don't hold back on her account."

I said, "Maybe we should split up, cover more area faster."

Mickey said, "That's a *wonderful* plan. I've been reading up on Private Dicks--" Hondo shook with silent laughter "--And you guys are *smart*, like Phillip Marlowe and Spenser and Travis McGee, just uncanny the way you work out what to do. Your minds are so *keen*, so piercing. I'm very impressed. I know you'll find Bob, I just know it." She teared up on the last part, but held it in.

I guess it never dawned on Mickey that the detectives she named weren't real flesh and blood people but hey, our minds were *keen*. I said, "Why don't you and Hondo take the long route and I'll take the short one, meet you back at the cars." Hondo tried to give me a look but he had his sunglasses on, so I acted like I didn't notice. Mickey didn't wait to discuss it, but hopped on her pink bike and started down the left trail. Hondo made a low noise like a dog's warning growl, then followed her.

I leaned my head back, looked at the hard blue sky above me and smiled. It's the little pleasures in life that are so satisfying. I eased onto my bike and started down the short trail, squirming on the seat as I went.

I'd gone maybe a hundred yards when I passed a small game trail on my left. I caught the light just right as I glanced at it and saw the faded impression of a bicycle tread. I stopped and looked at the narrow, threadlike path. It was maybe ten inches wide and curved around obstacles like a snake, slicing a pale line into the brush to disappear as it slanted behind a head-high slab of rock. I left the bike on the hiking trail and followed the faded bicycle impressions on foot. The tracks kept going as far as I could see, and the imprints were identical to my tires. I trotted back to the bike and turned it around. I rode as fast as I dared and it still took me ten minutes to catch up to Hondo and Mickey. I was so out of breath I couldn't even whisper when I got close enough to stop them.

Mickey hopped off her bike and hurried to me, all fluttering, touching hands and worried looks. "Are you all right? Are you having any chest pains, pains down the right arm -- or is it left? Are you having any pain down either arm?" Hondo put a hand on her shoulder and she stopped.

"You find something?" He said.

I nodded between gasps. Mickey hopped right in front of me, "I know what to do!" She made the peace sign with two fingers and tapped the V on her forearm. "Does it have two syllables?" She raised three fingers and tapped *them* on her forearm, "Three?"

Hondo said, "I don't think charades is what he had in mind. Let's give him a minute to catch his breath."

Mickey wrung her hands and bit at her lower lip and paced in tiny zigzags that always came back to me. I finally got enough air in my system to croak, "Found some tracks...on a game trail...same tread as ours."

Mickey hopped on her bike and showered dirt like a dragster as she took off. Hondo said, "Time to go, you athletic looking son of a gun."

Mickey passed up the game trail and we yelled at her. She skidded to a stop and pedaled back like an insane person. Her mohawk had mutated in all the wind and sweat so that it curled over to the side like Free Willy's dorsal fin. Pink and green glitter stuck to her face like fish scales and there were snail tracks where sweat trickled through the dust on her face. Fetching. "Where is it? Where's Bob? He's not hurt is he?"

"I don't know that it's even him. Calm down and we'll find out." We parked our bikes behind a large bush and started down the trail. Mickey was behind me moving constantly from side to side, peeking around my shoulder on the left side for five seconds, then my right, then left, over and over. I stopped. "Mickey, calm down or I'm going to tie you to a tree." Big tears formed in her eyes. *Christ.* I said, "Look, I'm sorry, but you need to be less noisy, move less on the trail. That will help us check this out faster. Can you do that?" The small head nodded, eyes big and red. A couple of pink flakes dropped off her cheek and fluttered to the ground. Mickey didn't say a word, but moved behind Hondo to take up the end of the line. Hondo mouthed, "You big bully," at me. I shook my head and turned to the tracks.

A hundred yards into the brush was a small side draw. A dense growth of oaks filled the bottom and several sycamores farther down indicated possible water. I caught the tiniest glimpse of yellow, like a fresh-discarded banana skin deep under the oaks. I pointed it out to Hondo and Mickey. "You see it?"

Hondo nodded and Mickey held my arm and jumped up and down, "Yesyesyes! You are so magnificent!" I got another look from Hondo.

We moved into the canyon and as we reached the bottom, the thick brush and young sapling oaks shortened our line of sight. Even so, we found a good trail that snaked around the thickest portions and moved under the big trees. The last bit of trail rounded a pile of large slabs of rock infused with marine fossils. I smelled smoke as we turned the corner and stepped into a small, neat clearing shaded by the largest oaks.

Two small brown women sat beside a fire and stared at us. From their facial expressions, you'd have thought we were a pack of man-eating lions. Mickey clung to my arm, then made a sound of alarm and pointed to a yellow bicycle leaning against a fallen log. "It's Bob's!"

She sprinted across the clearing and the women scrambled out of her path like frightened deer: afraid to run, afraid to stay. Mickey reached the bike and put her hands on it, alternately crying and cooing. You'd have thought it was a sacred relic.

Hondo told the aliens, "Amigos, amigos." He pointed to us as he talked. The women relaxed a little. They were around twenty, and had reddish-blond hair, green eyes and skin the color of caramel.

As we walked closer, we could see they were unkempt, with un-brushed hair and clothes they'd worn too long without laundering. These women had been living in the woods for a while. One of them had a bandage on her head, but seemed in no pain. They wore shorts and pullover tops, with one in tennis shoes and the other wearing Mexican sandals. Hondo said to Mickey, "You have a cell phone?"

"What? Yes, yes I do." She touched the bike one more time, then opened her purple fanny pack and took out a pink cell phone and walked to Hondo, putting it in his hand.

"It'll be long distance," he said.

"That's all right. Go ahead."

Hondo dialed a number and as it rang, he turned to me, "Figured I'd call Hunter and get her to translate for us. You want to talk to her?"

I shook my head, "Uh-uh. She's still mad at me."

Hondo's attention returned to the phone and he said, "Hey Hunter, It's Hondo. How you doing?" He listened for a few seconds and said, "Yeah, doing fine. Hey, Ronny's right here and he says Hi-" Hondo pulled the phone away from his ear, then put it back, "You bet. I'll be sure and tell him. Exactly, yes." He listened, then said, "I need to ask a favor. We are up in the mountains and ran into a couple of undocumented aliens, and they're young women, yes women, and we need to ask them some questions. They don't speak English and I thought you could translate for us." More listening, then, "Yes, I know you're working, but this is sort of like your business, after all you're the Border Patrol, right? The Border Patrol's for the whole United States, right, and California is part of that, right?" Hondo smiled and I knew Hunter Kincaid was laughing on the other end of the line. Hondo said, "Okay, I'll hand it to one of them, hold on." He walked to the woman who appeared the least nervous and showed her how to hold the phone. Hondo told Hunter, "I'm passing you over. Go ahead."

The small woman listened and nodded four or five times, never saying a word, then she suddenly jerked the phone away from her ear and looked at it wide-eyed. She put it back and said, "Si senorita official, voy a hablar!" The woman listened for a bit, then rattled off Spanish like a machine gun, using her free hand to emphasize the conversation as if Hunter could see as well as hear her.

She gave the phone to Hondo who listened, then said to Hunter, "We want to know about the bicycle they have. How they got it, when they got it, did they see anyone with it or nearby, did they hear anything that sounded like someone in trouble." Hondo handed the phone back to the woman, who listened, then talked for a long time, pointing at the sky and the ground and the other women who wore a dirty bandage on her ear and then back at the mountains.

She gave the phone back to Hondo, who listened for a while and said, "Okay, thanks a lot. We're going to call the Sheriff's office, let them know the women are here. The main thing is, they have a fire up here and everything's as dry as tinder. If the Santa Anas start blowing it'll burn all of these people to cinders and turn half the houses in Malibu to charcoal sticks. It's way too dangerous to let them stay. I have to tell you, though, I'd almost rather not do it." Hondo listened some more, then said, "Yeah, the case is a little funny, got some Hollywood people in it, so you could tag along and meet some movie stars."

I felt the hair raise up on my neck. What was he *doing*?

Hondo said, "Okay, we'll see you then. Adios." He handed the cell to Mickey and said to us, "Hunter said the women are from Durango, the city. They've been here for about two weeks. They were smuggled into the country by a coyote, an alien smuggler, a mean man who hid them near the highway. There were three others, but the – and I'm telling you what Hunter said they said – the beautiful man found them and brought them here. Three days ago, he came back while the two of them were out setting snares and he took the other three with him. They said he left a note in Spanish saying he would be back soon, but he hasn't returned. Hunter said she asked them what they had planned to do in the United States, and the woman said the coyote lied to them to get them across the border and then told them they would be forced to work as strippers and prostitutes."

"I don't like the sound of that."

Hondo said, "I know. Neither did Hunter. She's worried about them, said it sounds like a ring she worked in Florida that forced the women into prostitution and working at strip clubs. It's something we'll need to tell the Sheriff's office when we call."

Mickey said, "I don't see any food. What were they eating?"

"They were down to living on rabbits and a few tortillas until the miracle happened three days ago, the same day the other three women left with, we assume, Landman."

"Miracle?" Mickey said.

"That's what they called it. The woman said they were sitting around that evening talking about what to do when the bike fell from the sky and landed on Modesta's head. They considered it a miracle because now one of them can ride down to the edges of the communities and get food from dumpsters and bring it back."

I said, "It dropped from the sky?"

"Hunter said she quizzed her pretty close on that, and the woman said it absolutely came down on them from the air, that God in heaven must have seen their need and provided for them."

I thought about it for a minute as I checked the area. I looked at the location of the fire ring, then at the draw where we had entered, and tried to imagine where the biking trail was in relation to us. Hondo must have been reading my mind because he said, "I think the trail's pretty close to that ridge up there." He pointed to a higher outcrop that jutted at the top of a bluff on the hillside.

I said, "A strong guy could toss a bike off of there."

"I don't know. It's a long way out from there to the fire."

"Yeah, but I bet you could do it."

Hondo looked at it. "I could tell better from up there, but yeah, maybe."

In clothes, Hondo doesn't look muscular. In fact, he looks almost thin, even though he weighs about two-oh-five. But he's strong the way Bruce Lee was strong. I once watched Hondo pull a practical joke on a friend of ours where he took the friend's Volkswagen bug and put it in the bed of a nearby pickup truck.

He nudged me with his elbow. "Want to know what else Hunter said?"

"No, I do not."

He grinned, "She said she's got a vacation scheduled with no place to go, so I thought she might want to come visit, and she said she'd plan on coming out."

I closed my eyes, "Tell me you didn't."

"It'll be like old times."

"That's what I'm afraid of."

"Look at it this way: It'll give you a chance to work things out. You can't leave something like that unresolved."

"Thank you, Doctor Phil."

Mickey said, "Who's this Hunter Kincaid?"

Hondo said, "She's a friend of ours. Grew up in a town about twenty miles from Ronny and me. She and Ronny became quite the item last year while we were working a case, then they developed some problems that have to be worked out so we can all be friends again."

"She's a Border Patrol Agent?"

"Yeah, lives in West Texas. Good officer, too."

I said, "A hell of a shot. Deadly, not someone you want mad at you." I looked at Hondo as I spoke.

Mickey said, "I'd like to meet her. You know, Bob had optioned a script a couple of weeks ago that's about the Border Patrol. It's called Ninety Notches, and of course he would play the lead."

"Ninety Notches?"

Mickey pretended she was holding a pistol and she pointed at the grip. "You know, notches for the men killed in gunfights?"

If somebody lived through ninety gunfights and put notches in a pistol grip, there wouldn't be enough wood left to make a decent toothpick. The last person I'd read about who was vain enough to put notches on their gun was General Patton, and that had been when he was a young lieutenant with Pershing on their futile campaign into Mexico to find Pancho Villa.

Hondo said, "Sounds like an academy-award winner to me. That Bob is a genius at picking quality scripts. Big sense of realism with that one."

Mickey nodded her head, "That is exactly what he said: 'A movie about the realities of the border.'" As Mickey looked around you could see her mind returning to the realities of the present. She said, "What about Bob? He's not going to throw his favorite bike off a cliff. So what do we do now?"

"Why don't we go up there and take a look. There may not be anything to see, but we won't know if we don't look."

"What about Bob's bike?"

"We'll tell the sheriff's office about it when we call and have them bring it out. We can't take four bikes back without a lot of trouble."

We waved good-bye to the women and Mickey made push-down motions with her hands, saying in a loud, slow voice, "Stay-o...here-o." The women looked at her with eyes so big they reminded me of owls.

Hondo touched Mickey on the shoulder and as she looked at him, he shook his head and said, "No."

Hondo led us out of the draw and back up the trail. We reached a spot that came within fifty or sixty feet of the bluff. Hondo led us through the brush on a hand-wide trail made of flattened grass and broken twigs all the way to the edge of the bluff, where we looked down at the tops of the trees below. Just past the trees, the canyon deepened by five or six hundred feet. No sign of the women or their camp was visible.

I looked around, but the grass was so thick that nothing distinctive showed. I had my head down, focusing on the ground near the edge when Mickey squealed so loud I jumped and almost went over. "It's Bob's!"

I went to her and looked over the edge, then got to my hands and knees to grip the rock. Heights and me do not get along. Hondo came up behind and tapped the sole of my shoe with his toe, making a ha-ha gesture of kicking me off.

"That's *not* funny," I said. I think my voice quivered, but I'm not sure because I couldn't hear over the *thudthudthud* of my heart.

"You need to relax, let that tension flow out of you."

A laugh a minute, that's Hondo. He hopped over me to the edge and walked along it like walking across a gym floor. He spotted it at the same time I did. A purple fanny pack, exactly like the one Mickey wore, hung up on a small bush growing out of the bluff twenty feet below the rim.

I started to say something to Hondo, but he had disappeared. As I got to my feet, Mickey screamed near my ear, "Don't fall!" My heart whanged against my ribcage.

"Don't *do* that." I said. She was biting her fingers and pointing down the edge of the cliff. Hondo was free-climbing down the rocks like a spider, with nothing but a pair of cotton shorts between him and a hundred foot fall to rocks.

We watched him, with Mickey clinging to me the way a baby spider monkey clings to its mother. I was beginning to worry about the circulation in my arm when Hondo reached the fanny pack, picked it up, put it over his arm and neck like a bandoleer, and started up. He came up faster than he went down. When he topped out, he handed the fanny pack to Mickey. His fingers left pale dusty prints on the purple cloth. Mickey opened it and moaned. "It's his. It's really his. What do we do now?" She looked like she was going to cry.

"Let me take a look," I said. She handed it to me and I squatted down, dumping out the contents on the pale yellow grass. There was a stick of strawberry Chapstick, a granola bar, a half-full box of Tic-Tacs, a money clip with the initials B.L. holding a half-inch thick stack of folded hundreds, a cheap pen from a Motel Camino Real with an address in East LA, some scraps of paper, a Leatherman pocket tool, and two flint arrowheads.

"Chumash," Hondo said.

"What?"

"The arrowheads. They're Chumash. Lived in these mountains for thousands of years."

"Thank you, Professor Leakey." I turned to Mickey, who was about to cry again, "Mickey, did Bob collect arrowheads?"

"No, not that I ever saw."

I puzzled over it, then started looking at the scraps of paper, turning them with a broken stem of grass. There were several numbers written on individual pieces, and the last one had a jumble of words. "Bingo," I said. Hondo and Mickey looked over my shoulder and read: *Valdar Deco Urgent Paint Martinez Chumash*. There had been something written after Chumash, but the paper was torn and all that was left was a bow-shaped line that could have been the start of anything. I thought maybe an O or a C.

Hondo reached over and pointed at the word Chumash, then stood up and grinned. "Knowledge is power," he said.

This was enough for me. I borrowed Mickey's cell phone and called my friend, Vick Best with the Sheriff's department. I thought our location was county jurisdiction and things were not looking rosy for Bob Landman. I told Vick where we were.

He said, "We'll be right out, don't go anywhere."

I told the others and we sat down to wait. It was an hour before the deputies showed up on four-wheelers. We talked it through and the deputies went into the draw to talk to the women and to put out any coals in the fire ring. Sergeant Vick Best said to Hondo and me, "You two going to Texas any time soon?"

"I don't think so," I said.

"You do talk to people back there, right?"

"Sure."

"Okay, it'll square us up if you get them to send a care package this way."

"Like what?"

"Last time I went through Texas near San Antonio I ate some local chips and salsa that were almost addictive. About three big bags of Julio's chips and three jars of his salsa would be just fine."

Hondo said, "I can eat a bag of those in about five seconds."

"Tell me about it." Vick looked around and said, "It'll be official now, we'll list Landman as a Missing Person. We're going to be a while up here, but you three can leave. We'll take the women in, get them cleaned, and fed, then call immigration. If it's like last time, they'll tell us to turn them loose because they don't have anybody that can come. We'll probably hold these women for a couple days just to get a few meals into them." He shook his head. You three go on, now. I know where to reach you."

Mickey said, "And you'll deliver Bob's bike?"

"We will. Don't worry about a thing. Now go, you all look bushed."

**

By the time we rode back to the cars, Mickey had convinced us to stop at Landman's home and rest a bit. We loaded the bikes and followed Mickey to the house and through the massive doors to a large entertainment room. I was starving and asked Mickey, "Do you think Bob would mind if we raided his kitchen?" She told us to stay, then scurried into the kitchen, eager to have something to do. Hondo and I sunk into two of the huge, comfortable chairs arranged in a semi-circle facing an enormous plasma screen television hung on the wall.

Hondo said, "What do you make of those other words and names, the way they were all jumbled together? They were arranged like a pile of rocks."

"Beats me. We'll just start with what we can figure out, and that's Valdar."

Hondo said, "Yeah, probably not too many Chumash around to ask."

Mickey came back, pushing a food cart with assorted cold cuts, vegetables, cheeses, crackers, chips, sliced fruit, four types of dips, and showcased in the center was a plastic cylinder full of individually wrapped pieces of dried meat. The wrappers read: *Kataki's Gourmet Kobi Beef Jerky.*

I pointed at the jerky and raised my eyebrows. Mickey said, "Bob receives cases of it every month from Japan. He did a commercial for it over there. It's a big seller."

Next to the jerky was an iced magnum of Cristal champagne, china plates, knives and forks, cloth napkins and three glasses.

Hondo said, "You whip all this up just now?"

Mickey blushed and turned her head, "It was nothing. I like doing it for you two."

I looked at the champagne, "Bob likes this?"

"Oh my, yes. He has several cases of it in the wine cellar. It's his favorite."

We nibbled on the jerky, which was better than most steaks I'd eaten in restaurants, and relaxed and drank champagne until the bottle was empty. Mickey sprang from her seat as if a catapult launched her and hurried into the kitchen, returning with a second bottle. We drank that, too. Hondo mentioned something about not wanting to offend the host. After the third bottle I was feeling no pain. Hondo said that if we drank one more, he'd be at Stage Ten on Dan Jenkins' Ten Stages of Drunkenness, which is: Crank Up The Enola Gay.

We left Mickey at Landman's where she planned to spend the night. As we left, Mickey said, "I may check out some things tomorrow, do some investigating."

"Why don't you tell us what it is and we'll do it. That's what we're getting paid to do."

She shook her head, "No, no I'll do it. Makes me feel like I can make a difference. I'll do my sleuthing inconspicuously, don't worry."

Now she was using words like sleuthing. "Don't get into any trouble, Mickey. If you even dream it's dangerous, you call me, okay?"

She nodded and almost fell through the huge doorway as her head went forward. She grabbed my belt to keep from falling. "I guess I had a little too mush to drink. I think I'll go to bed now." She closed the big marble door and we walked to the Mercedes.

"You want to drive?" Hondo asked.

"Heck no I don't want to drive. I had too much champagne."

"Me too."

"Then you better drive careful, and slow, and don't bother me because I'll be asleep in the passenger seat."

Hondo didn't say anything and we drove off.

CHAPTER FOUR

I woke to the sounds of many honking horns. I opened one eye and looked along the back of the convertible. Cars were stacked bumper to bumper in two lines that went back a quarter-mile. No one could pass because the Mercedes was straddling the middle stripe.

I looked over at Hondo and saw he was smiling, wearing his shades and humming along as the Mamas and Papas sang *California Dreaming* from the speakers. "You realize you're blocking two lanes of traffic?"

"Sure."

I waited for more. There was only silence, humming. "You want to tell me why?" I said.

"I noticed everyone passing seemed angry and in a hurry. I thought I could slow things down, let them re-adjust their karma and mellow out. It's too beautiful an afternoon to have so many angry vibes permeating the highway populace."

I started laughing, "Sometimes I wonder if you're not a hippie who got zapped here in a time warp. Some of these people may be in a legitimate hurry. Some of them may be armed with AK's. You need to let them pass," I shook my head. "Next thing I know you'll be wearing love beads and have flowers poking out of your hair."

Hondo gave me the peace sign, pulled over and waved for the next ten minutes as cars passed, honking their horns and yelling and shooting us the finger. California, land of mellow. When most of them had passed, Hondo sped up and got me home without either of us being shot or maimed by irate drivers.

I checked my phone for messages and had none, went to the bedroom, showered and changed into fresh gym shorts, then checked my e-mail. There were a few jokes sent to me by friends, but nothing extraordinary. I shut it off and went to the living room to catch the local evening news.

One thing about drinking early and then taking a short nap and waking, it left me with a dull headache, fuzzy thinking and a cranky disposition. You'd think I would learn. I went to the kitchen and drank two large glasses of water, dug through the refrigerator and found half a Papa John's Canadian bacon and pineapple pizza and several Rolling Rocks. I took one of the beers and the pizza and went to the couch.

As I ate the cold pizza, I thought about where in the hell Bob Landman could be. Things, especially considering what we found today, were not pointing in a good direction.

The Mexican women hadn't heard a thing when Bob's bike was thrown from the cliff, which indicated to me that Landman himself had thrown the bike and fanny pack, or he had been rendered unable to call out, or the bike and fanny pack had been taken from him on the trail, too far from the edge for the women to hear a yell or scuffle.

I ate a second slice of pizza and drank a second beer, which seemed to help my headache and disposition. The news was long over and I flipped channels through all nine thousand stations twice before stopping on the Discovery Channel and a special on Neanderthals.

I ate the last slice of pizza and was on the last beer when the doorbell rang. I almost didn't get up because the show was where the Cro-Magnons -- baldheaded guys with dried flaky clay on their faces -- were about to whomp up on the poor Neanderthals. I wanted to see *my* team win, feel good for a change. The bell rang again and I went to the door and looked through the peep hole.

Bond Meadows stood there wearing an open, knee-length fur coat and black stiletto heels and nothing else, unless you counted the bottle of Cristal champagne in her hand. On seeing the bottle, I pondered opening the door. She rang again and I peeked again. Maybe I only had the strength of seven or eight tonight. I opened the door and she came in.

"I thought you were never going to open the door."

"I wanted to see how you were holding that bottle before I did."

A flash went through her eyes, then faded. "That's not very nice."

"What do you want?"

She shed the coat, then kicked off her high heels and walked to the couch to sit down. He body was incredible. The only other one even close was Hunter Kincaid, but in a more athletic way. Bond opened the champagne with a pop and said, "Do you have two glasses?"

I nodded instead of speaking because my tongue had turned to stone. Other body parts were following the tongue.

"Well, go get the glasses, silly boy."

I went to the kitchen and returned with two jelly glasses, the last clean glasses in the house.

She took one, "The Flintstones, very avant-garde." She poured the glass half-full and handed it to me, then poured her own. She patted the couch beside her and said, "Sit down so we can talk."

I was *so* aware that I only had on a pair of gym shorts. She moved closer and I felt her naked leg press against mine from hip to knee. The hairs on my exposed thigh tingled and stood higher. She ran a hand across them, trailed her nails up my hip and to the back of my neck, playing with the hairs. Goosebumps popped up on my arms. My breathing was heavy and the smell of her made my head spin. "Drink your champagne," she said.

I drank. I turned my head to look at her face, but my eyes were trying to grow out on stalks like a crab's so I could angle them down and ogle this close, naked, perfect body without Bond realizing I wasn't looking at her face. The thought of it reminded me of being sixteen and in the back of a car. I felt a small grin start, then grow wider as I thought about it, then I started laughing.

Bond moved away from me and frowned. "What's so funny?"

I couldn't stop. I tried to explain, but burst out laughing each time. One thing about laughing like that, it's contagious. Before I knew it, Bond was chuckling, and then laughing along with me. We went on like that until our sides ached and we tapered off, with occasional hysterical flare-ups that had us wiping our cheeks.

When we stopped for good and caught our breath I said, "What are you doing here, and what's with the seduction?"

Without our laughing jaunt, we'd be rutting on the carpet and furniture like a pair of supercharged minks, that I knew.

"I wanted to make sure you were on my side."

"You don't have to screw me to get that. If something happens to change it, I'll tell you." I sipped some Cristal and said, "Who did you think I'd side with?"

"Frank."

I snorted, "Frank? He may be your husband but he's an ass."

"Well, he's a powerful man, and powerful men get what they want."

"Not always." I took another sip and wiped off a drop running across Barney Rubble. "Did Frank say something to you?"

"He hinted that you were working for him, that he'd hired you from under whoever originally hired you. He doesn't know it's me, and I thank you for keeping it from him."

I drained my glass and walked to the kitchen sink where I rinsed the glass and looked at her across the open bar that separated the living room from the kitchen. I said, "If Frank was here I'd tell him right to his face-" the door burst open and Carl Rakes stepped in, followed by Frank Meadows.

"You'd tell Frank what?" Frank said as he rubbed his hands over his knuckles. He looked at Bond and said, "Put some clothes on, bitch."

Now wasn't this a fine way to end an evening? Carl stood to the side of the door with his hands on his hips. He was dressed in a black fishnet tee shirt, tight-fitting black leather pants and lace-up work boots. His arms and torso were covered in blue-black prison tattoos. There were skulls and pirates, church cupolas, a portrait of Madonna, one-hundred dollar bills on each pec, and lots of words and phrases with some of the letters looking like backwards E's and R's and upside down V's. The indigo ink highlighted Carl's muscles like oil on a bodybuilder. His chest and stomach looked hard enough to break a knife blade. Frank said, "Carl, get that sonofoabitch over here."

You'd think he might ask me to walk over, after all it was my house. When Carl reached the end of the bar I slipped my hand into the sink and grabbed the handle of a meat tenderizing mallet I'd used the night before on a round steak. It was solid aluminum with a handle like a hammer and a head the size of a coke can. The face of the mallet was a pattern of small pyramids, almost like the inside of a waffle maker. Carl didn't see me hide it behind my leg, and as he came around the bar I made my move.

Carl was fast and leaned back from what he thought was a spinning backfist, but I faked with it and followed around with the mallet and its extra fourteen inches of length and caught him dead center in the middle of the forehead.

There was a loud *thock* and I felt the impact all the way to my shoulder. Carl dropped in a heap and his body started jerking and quivering. Hondo calls it "Doing the chicken".

I walked around the bar and said, "Frank, you get this piece of trash out of my house and if you ever come in again, I'll shoot your sorry ass."

Frank rubbed his hands harder, like he couldn't wash something off, "You wait, Baca. You don't have a clue what you're getting into."

He started to say something to Bond, who still hadn't put on any clothes but I said, "Uh-uh. She stays. Now get him out of here before I call the cops."

Frank went to Carl and helped him up. The mark of the meat mallet was glowing on Carl's forehead like a fresh red brand. Tiny pinheads of blood caught the lights and glinted in the deepest parts of the waffle marks like miniature red Christmas bulbs. He wobbled beside Frank to the door and they went out without closing it.

I walked to the door and saw the latch was broken, so moved a chair against it.

Bond said, "Do you mean it? I can stay?"

"For a while. You don't need to go home and be around him."

I sat on the couch and she slid beside me. She touched my face and moved hers so close I felt the soft breath of her words, "Then we won't laugh this time."

**

When I woke the next morning Bond was asleep with only the top of her head above the covers. I rose and showered, put on fresh Wranglers, gray New Balance shoes, a black polo, my shoulder holster and my gray, fresh-from-the-cleaners Patagonia windbreaker. I let myself out without making a sound. The drive to the office left me time to think. Bond jumping into bed with me was unexpected but not unique, especially in Los Angeles where people still seemed to have sex as easy as shaking hands. Maybe I should have said no.

Nahh, who was I kidding? The woman caught me at a weak moment and that was that. At least that was what I was going to tell myself.

Thoughts about Frank were different. I wasn't sure if he followed Bond to the house, but that would be the logical thing, especially since he showed no surprise at her being there. But Frank's last words, "You don't have a clue what you're getting into," nagged at me. That, and the fact he sent Carl after me without much talk. It shouldn't have been his play. Too many chances to sue, especially when it was in my own house.

I parked in the gym's lot and went to my office. Hondo was already there and had a fresh cup of coffee waiting on my desk. He was sipping out of his favorite Star Wars mug and making origami with his free hand. There were two bird things on his desk and now he was working on what looked like a dog.

I'm more refined. I drank from a personalized mug given to me by Hunter Kincaid. On one side it had a picture of Hannibal Lecter in his leather mask above two sugar cubes. On the other it read in Halloween letters: *The Silence of the Lumps*. I also ate a bag of peanut M&M's. Between the coffee and the chocolate, I thought I might get enough caffeine. The peanuts were for nutrition.

"I had a visit from Frank and Carl last night."

Hondo's eyebrows went up. "He wanting you to co-star with Tom Cruise?"

I filled him in and waited until the last to mention that Bond had spent the night. He looked at me and said, "Freud would have a field day with you."

We were both drinking a second cup of coffee when Hondo said, "So, what are you going to do when Hunter shows up tomorrow?"

I burned my tongue and sat up. "She's really coming?"

"Yep. She won't say it, and neither will you, but you both want to be friends again."

I nodded, "Yeah. We never should have taken it that far. We were great as friends."

"You can get it back. But Bond may be a problem. Might be like rubbing Hunter's nose in it or something. Your call, though."

I nodded and thought about things as we finished our coffee. After we rinsed our cups and got in my truck, we headed for Landman's house in Malibu to find Valdar, the painter. On the way, Sergeant Vick called to tell us that luminal tests on Landman's fanny pack were negative: no evidence of blood. I asked him about prints off the money clip or anything else and he said partials in several places but nothing with enough points to identify. Vick also said the phone numbers on the sheets of paper had been the offices of several film companies, that they'd called and noted that Landman was friends with some of the producers and called on occasion to chat, and that no one had heard from Landman in four or five days. He reminded me about the Julio's chips and salsa and hung up.

We reached Landman's Malibu address twenty minutes later and parked at the edge of the road. The sound of surf rumbled and the smell of the ocean was fresh and clean as we walked to the door and rang the bell. No one answered, so we went down the ridge to the ocean side of the house and saw an open sliding patio door on the second floor deck. I yelled a few times, but got no answer. Hondo went to the privacy gate on the stairs and after a moment said, "It's open, let's go."

I followed him up and we went through the patio door. Fine sand gritted as we stepped in and curtains floated in the breeze like the arms of banshees.

There were canvases in various sizes and in various stages of completion littering the floor and leaning against the wall. One large canvas on an easel was half complete and showed Bob Landman as a Border Patrol Agent with gun belt and western Stetson looking out over mountains from a rocky point that seemed familiar.

"That's where the bike went over," Hondo said.

There was a color photo printed on computer paper attached to the side of the canvas, which showed Landman posing, sans uniform, like the painting and standing on the lip of the cliff where we'd stood yesterday. At the edge of the photo was a portion of yellow bicycle showing, the Colnago, and on the far side of it was a foot and leg in jeans to the knee. Someone else was with him.

"Let's look for a camera or see if he's got a computer with the pictures already loaded."

Hondo walked into the bedroom as I moved down the hallway. I hadn't taken three steps before Hondo said, "Better come in here, Ronny."

At first, I thought it was red paint, but then the smell kicked in and I recognized it as blood. Blood everywhere: splattered on the wall, the bed, the floor, and smeared across the sliding mirrored doors of the closet. Whoever was bleeding had struggled in a fight that ranged around the room. There were prints on the floor showing what looked like four shoes of different sizes, and there were prints of one person's bare feet.

"You bring your cell with you?" Hondo asked.

"Yeah, but I don't think we want to call the police on it. Probably should make an anonymous call from a pay phone so we don't get asked how we got inside." I looked around and said, "Besides, they don't have to hurry. Whoever lost this much blood doesn't need an ambulance, they need a hearse."

A muffled squeal came from behind the mirrored closet doors. We looked at each other and Hondo went to the closet with his Glock in his hand, being careful not to step in any of the drying blood. He slid open the door.

A small, crying figure wearing a black turtleneck sweater and black stretch pants, black tennis shoes and a black watch cap came scooting out of the dark. The watch cap hung on a clothes hanger and jerked off the figure's head, revealing blond, spikey hair that must have been styled with a rake.

Mickey ran to me and buried her face in my chest before I could remove my windbreaker. She cried and sobbed and sniffled for five minutes before raising her head and smiling through clown makeup. "I'm so glad to see you two. I was sooo scared."

I glanced at my Patagonia and figured I might have to burn it this time. I said, "What are you doing here?"

She sniffled and we moved her from the bedroom to the living room. I watched Hondo check her shoes as she walked and he shook his head to tell me there wasn't any blood on them. We sat at a glass table with tubular brass chairs around it and Mickey told us what she'd seen.

**

"I was sleuthing the area last night, wanting to eyeball what Valdar was working on, see if he had any dames or bimbos casing the joint, when I saw him slip the house and go for a walk down the beach. I didn't have a roscoe, so I was being careful. When he was far enough away I used my bins and scoped the pad for perps, then sleuthed in through the door and began detecting."

I said, "Mickey, *please* use regular words. I only got a D in Private Eye Talk one-oh-one."

"Oh all right. But you should have studied more." She took a breath and continued, "I looked at his paintings and things, then saw the photo attached to the canvas on the easel. It was the place we were yesterday, above where the Mexican women had been sitting by the fire.

"Well, that got me interested and I sleuthed, uh, looked around some more and was in his bedroom when I heard Valdar in the living room. I didn't know what to do so I got in the closet and closed the doors. I hid behind the clothes and listened for what seemed like hours. It had been quiet for a while and I thought that maybe he was gone, so I stepped out. I was almost to the door when I heard the patio door slide open and Valdar said, 'What are you doing here?'" Mickey wiped her hands on her thighs as she recalled the events. "I hopped back into the closet and could hear muffled voices, several of them, and they all sounded angry, even Valdar's. Then I heard a yell and some running and everyone was in the bedroom and there was the sound of hitting and fighting and a couple of times I heard a voice yell out in pain."

She began to tear up and I told her, "It's over now. You're just being a good detective and giving us the facts."

She nodded, "It went on for a while and finally there was a thump and some gasps and then quiet. Someone out there said something in a language I didn't know, then I heard some grunts and steps leaving, and I heard them take the computer because they banged it against the wall when they moved it. But they all didn't go. A couple of them stayed in the house. I could hear them turning on the television and doing things in the kitchen, and one of them came in here and lay on the bed. He went to sleep because I could hear him snoring."

"So you were here all night."

"Yes."

"What time did they leave this morning?"

"I don't know the time, but it was maybe three hours before you two got here." She shook her head, "I wasn't going to leave that closet for anything. Some people came back about two hours later and they all talked in the living room, then moved in the bedroom and talked some more before they left. They haven't been gone more than fifteen minutes or so."

Hondo said, "Did it sound like they were looking for something? Could you hear anything like that?"

"Yes, like I said, the first ones banged everything around and took the computer. The men in the second group that came this morning were different. They opened drawers and things, but were very careful. I could hear them close things back, put stuff back in place."

"They didn't check the closet?"

"Oh yes. I was behind some long Armani jackets and held my breath when they opened the door. I just knew they would find me, but they only moved a few clothes and looked on the top shelf, where they took a box of some kind, and closed the door."

"Do you know what type of box?"

"I think it was a shoe box, but I'm not sure. The clothes moved when the guy took it down and I caught a glimpse of his hand and part of the box."

"Did the hand have any tattoos, any rings?"

"No, it was brown looking, like maybe a medium skinned Hispanic or somebody from the Mediterranean, that kind of brown. There weren't any rings or tattoos that I remember."

"Could you guess how tall he was?"

"Over six feet, I know that, because he blocked out a lot of the closet light."

Hondo said, "Why don't we leave, stop at a payphone and make the call to the police. I think whoever did this got what they wanted."

Mickey squirmed, "Okay, but first I have to pee. I've been holding it all night." She hurried into the bathroom, holding herself all the way. While she was gone, I went to the easel, took the photo of Landman, and put it inside my shirt.

We left after checking to see that it was clear. We drove Mickey to her car, dropped her off and told her to go home and stay there, then we drove until we found a payphone and I called the police. I used a Spanish accent and told them I wouldn't give my name because I was an illegal.

We returned to the office and Hondo ground the last of the Jamaican Blue Mountain and made coffee. We poured our cups and sat at the desks, sipping and thinking. I debated telling Bond about the blood, but decided if I wasn't going to tell the police, I wouldn't tell her.

Hondo had the photo I'd taken and was studying it. "We need to take this, get it blown up."

"You see something?"

"I'm not sure, but I think we might make out the shoe type on this phantom leg, and it looks like there's something else beside the foot, but it's in shadow and I can't make it out."

I sipped some coffee and said, "Wish we'd had time to go through the computer or found a camera."

"Yeah, but that would be the *easy* way. We don't want it easy, that's no fun."

"For you, maybe. Me, I like easy."

The phone rang and I punched the conference button so Hondo and I could both hear. Sergeant Best was on the line. "You make a call to the police this morning, telling about a room full of blood at Bob Landman's beach house?"

"Well good morning to you too, Vick."

"Funny thing, the detective I talked to said it was an illegal alien made the call. Me, I don't believe in coincidence and what with you and I recently discussing Landman's disappearance becoming a law enforcement matter, I thought I'd check with you, make sure you know it's against the law to break and enter, to disturb evidence at a crime scene, among other things."

"I realize that Sergeant Best, sir. You can be assured my partner and I know those things are against the law."

We could hear Vick tapping a pencil on his desk. He said, "That's what I figured, smartass. Stay out of the way on this Ronny. You or Hondo screw up and I'll haul your asses to jail for interfering in an investigation."

"That's clear enough."

"I gotta go, the Governor created a frigging thirty man task force with someone from every department in greater LA on it, supposed to look into Landman's disappearance and we've got a press conference in ten minutes."

"Are you heading it up?"

"Yes, dammit."

"Well congrats there, Sergeant Best."

"Screw you, and get me my chips or I'm gonna be pissed."

I punched the phone button off and said, "You think he needs the Julio's for a tranquilizer, or is it just comfort food?"

"He's been a little high strung ever since you shot him last year."

"Hey, that's not fair, he moved."

The corner of Hondo's mouth went up the tiniest bit and we sat in silence finishing our coffee.

CHAPTER FIVE

Hondo was looking at the pen and the words list he had lifted from Bob Landman's purple fanny pack when he said, "Want to get out of here, go check a few things?"

"Like what?"

He held up the cheap pen, "This motel's in East LA"

"Sure, what car?"

"I think Shamu'll work best."

We drove through the barrios and looked at the gang graffiti marking territorial boundaries. The Maravilla and White Fence gangs were in the area, and the Camino Real was located on their borderline. I parked near the front of the hotel and followed Hondo into the lobby where a tall, thin redheaded man with severely crossed pale eyes stood behind the counter and watched us enter — at least I think he watched us enter, but his gaze was somewhere between Hondo and me.

Hondo leaned on the counter and said, "Get many Hollywood stars in here?"

He said, "You mean like Elvis?"

I looked at him.

Hondo said, "More like living ones."

The redhead moved both hands to his head and massaged his temples while his eyes squinted shut. After ten seconds, he opened them and said, "Had Lassie in here once. She had a good time, too."

I said, "How about Bruce Willis, Tom Cruise, Bob Landman, those guys."

"Oh sure, Landman was in here last week. Been in three, four times this month. I didn't know you meant actors, I thought you said stars."

How do you argue with that? I said, "Did Landman come in alone?"

He rubbed his head again for several seconds, then said, "No sir."

"Do you remember who was with him?"

"Don't know their names."

I said, "How about what they looked like, can you describe them?"

"Uh-huh."

Silence.

"*Would* you describe them?"

"Sure."

Silence.

I said, "Right now. Would you describe them right now?" Dentists didn't have this much trouble pulling a wisdom tooth.

He appeared testy, "Why didn't you say so, instead of beating around the bush?" He fiddled with a pen on the counter and sulked for a bit, then said, "There were two of them with him last week, a man and a woman." He suddenly got a suspicious look on his face and said, "You aren't with the newspaper are you?"

"No."

"Okay then. Good, because the papers are full of trash, except for the Enquirer. They know Elvis is still alive and the saucers bring him back to earth regular so he can visit. Now that's real news if you ask me. Sayy, if you're with the Enquirer—"

I looked around like I was making sure we were alone. "We are, and you're pretty darn sharp to catch on like that. In fact, I wrote that Elvis article, met the King himself."

He grinned and said, "I knew it!"

"It's between us, okay?" He nodded and I said, "Now, can you describe the man and woman?"

"Sure, the man was tall, kinda scary looking, had long hair. The woman now, she was a looker, I tell you. That one is somebody's trophy wife or girlfriend."

"Did the tall man have any tattoos?"

"He had on a coat, and I didn't see any."

"Was the woman dark, light, blond, brunette?"

"She was built like a brick shithouse," he held his hands cupped in front of his chest, "I mean like big firm melons. I didn't pay much attention to her hair, but I think it was kinda red, maybe."

"How long did they stay?"

"I don't know."

"Could you look?"

"Yeah, I guess so." He punched numbers on the computer and said, "Huh, that's funny. His name's not on here."

Hondo said, "Maybe he used an assumed name, or one of the others checked in for him."

"No, I remember exactly, because he didn't use Bob, he used Robert." He punched keys again and frowned at the screen. "I don't understand."

I said, "Did he sign something?"

"Yeah, he did. I'll have to go dig through the hard copies from last week, but he did sign. Signed Robert Landman, I remember it."

His nametag read Loomis. I said, "Loomis, we'll come around tomorrow and check with you. Here's something for your trouble, and we'll match it tomorrow if you find us anything good." I handed him a hundred dollar bill.

He took it, looked around and put it in his pocket. "You fellows come here after one. I'll be by myself then."

We nodded and as Hondo pushed the door to go out, we heard Loomis hissing, "Tell Elvis hello for me!"

When we got outside, I could see three Hispanics leaning on the driver's side door of my pickup. They appeared to be in their early twenties and were dressed in baggy khakis, white undershirts, and were drinking forties of malt liquor, holding them at their sides by putting a finger in the mouth of the bottle.

We stopped at the truck and they didn't move. "Excuse me guys, this is my truck."

The one wearing the hairnet said, "Truck? I thought it was a fish." They all ha-ha'd and still didn't move.

Hondo took his sunglasses off and hooked them on his belt, pulling his jacket out and away from his underarm to make room. He said, "I tell him all the time it looks like Shamu."

Hairnet said, "Yeah, that's the one. Man, when you gonna get a real paint job on this bruto? This is a big, bad-ass truck, gringo."

I could see the butts of handguns sticking out of the pants of the closest two, so I had to guess all three were armed. I gave an aw-shucks smile and eased a half-step at a forty-five degree angle to settle into an Open Bi-Jong stance they wouldn't recognize as anything. It left no soft areas exposed and opened my jacket an inch away from my side. The magnum's weight against my ribs was telling my hand right where to go.

Hairnet grinned at us and pulled out a switchblade, flicking the button. As he started to rake the point across the side of the truck, Hondo shook his head and said, "Uh-uh."

At that same moment, I felt the hair on my neck prickle and I turned to look behind us at the street. A lowrider was coming by with two cholos hanging out of the windows, holding Mac-10s in each hand. I yelled and the others glanced at the street. I was already moving and Hondo was a heartbeat behind as we tackled the three boys and shoved them to the pavement while the four Macs *bratted* nine-millimeter bullets into the side of Shamu at a rate of twenty-five rounds per second. It sounded like being under a metal shed during a bad hailstorm for two seconds, then their magazines were empty and it was silent.

When we heard the car speed away, Hondo and I got off the three gangbangers, who were much slower getting up. Hairnet was holding his arm where Hondo had hit him to knock him down.

"Man, *es-say*, you almost broke it."

"I thought about holding you in front of the truck to save the paint job."

Shamu had lots of holes in the sides and a wavy string of spiderwebs in the front window. The angled glass had caused the nine millimeters to ricochet off rather than penetrate.

Hairnet talked to the other two in Spanish, then said, "I'm not complaining man, it's just that I never been hit like that. My neck hurts and my teeth clicked together so hard I got tiny chips in my mouth." He looked at me, "How you know they was coming?"

"I felt it. Nothing else I can tell you."

"Like a psychic thing, uh? That's cool, man. What's your names?"

"I'm Ronny Baca, He's Hondo Wells."

"Both of you got Spanish in your names, that's good."

I could hear sirens in the distance. On a hunch I said, "You three get out of here, we'll take care of the cops."

Hairnet looked at us for a second, then said, "You saved the lives of three Maravillas, and it's not something we forget. If you need anything, you ask for one of us. My name is Pretty Boy, this is Chato and he's Cuarenta."

"Forty?" Hondo said.

Pretty Boy said, "Yeah, he likes his beer." That was it. They trotted off and disappeared around the corner. Two minutes later a police vehicle pulled up and the officers got out. We told them our story of innocence, of walking to our vehicle and this car drove by and we saw the guns just in time. They had us go over it three times before they were satisfied.

As they were leaving Hondo asked them, "Is he going to get stopped for driving his truck like this?"

The older officer said, "No, but he'll get a lot of looks."

The officer was right.

**

I dropped Hondo at his car and had him follow me to the local garage. The body man wiped his hands on a red rag and said, "You take a left through a firing range?"

Everybody's a comedian. I said, "Can you fix it up?"

"I can if the store's got enough Bond-O, that's a lot of holes. The windows are no problem and nothing hit the engine, so you're okay there. You want me to paint over that white so it doesn't look like a fish?"

"It's not a fish, it's a mammal."

"You want me to paint it all black or not?"

I had a chance to end the ridicule, but this was becoming a point of honor. "Paint it like it was," I said.

Hondo grinned, shook his head and walked to the Mercedes.

At the office, we decided we should split up and work two things at once. Hondo would go to Landman's office and get with Mickey to go over records for the weeks preceding Bob's disappearance, and I was going to check around on the Valdar connection. Hondo left and I went through the side door and into the gym. My friend was behind the juice bar drinking something that looked like a half-gallon purple milkshake.

"Arch, what is that?" I asked.

Archie swallowed and grimaced at the taste, "My own recipe. Keeps me going all day."

I said, "You know, at your age prunes will keep you going all day, too." Archie was eighty years old, a bodybuilder from the golden age of Muscle Beach who'd placed second in contests a half-dozen times to Steve Reeves and John Grimek. He still does a thousand sit-ups a day and can bench press three-fifty. Archie bought the building thirty years ago and had part of it converted into an apartment, where he now lived, and the remainder into a gym and our office. Archie finished the drink in six huge swallows, burped and said, "You must want something with all that flattery you're throwing at me."

I put my hand over my heart, "Archie, how can you say that?"

"Your ass. Now, what do you need?"

"My truck's in the shop-"

"What's the matter, it get harpooned?" Oh, he thought that was funny.

"Nooo. I'm having a little body work done, so I don't have any wheels."

He walked to the front desk, reached behind the counter and pulled out some keys. He tossed them to me and said, "The Vette's around back. Don't wreck it."

Archie's Corvette is a mint condition, candy apple red sixty-three convertible. He'd bought it new after some friends got him speaking parts in several of those late fifties-early sixties motorcycle gang movies.

It was a fine feeling to drive along Santa Monica Boulevard with the top down. I slowed as I passed the Beverly Hilton, getting waves and smiles from three young women getting into a Bentley. I took a left on Wilshire and a few minutes later passed Sotheby's and turned onto Dayton Way. Pelson's Galleries, LLC was up on the right and I parked beside a baby blue convertible Ferrari 360 Modena Spider. On days like this, convertibles seemed to sprout like mushrooms.

Inside, I told a willowy young man with blinding white teeth who I was and asked him to tell Harold Pelson, the owner, that I would like to have a minute with him.

Harold came out and shook my hand as he led me to his office. We exchanged the usual pleasantries and I got to the reason for my visit.

"What can you tell me about an artist named Valdar?"

Harold pursed his lips, thought a moment and said, "I read something the other day about possible foul play. I believe it said there was blood found in the home he was living in at Malibu."

"I read it, too. But what I'm interested in is his history, that sort of thing."

"Well, he's originally from the former Soviet Union, a town on the Volga River called Samara, where the Samara and Volga join. He was discovered while working at the big prison there, and he developed a quick following in Europe and over here. He made his first show in the United States three years ago, in New York. It was some of his best work, very primitive and powerful. He's gaining fame because of his outlaw personality and raw talent. But he's very uneven. I've seen several of his paintings that were extraordinary, very bold and powerful, and others that look like they should have been painted on velvet and sold in Mexico."

"That bad."

"Yes. He seems to get caught up in other styles, and then butchers them when he paints. Absolutely atrocious, and he doesn't take criticism well at all. But then, that also adds to his mystique. He's a rough man, and has been in a number of serious brawls with people who don't see things his way."

"You mean like fistfights?"

"Yes."

"I don't normally associate artists with that type behavior."

"There are a few bad ones; egotists, boors, womanizers, drunkards, hedonists. But you're right; artists are not normally people who beat others to a bloody mess."

"Have you met him while he's been in California?"

"I was at the same party once. It was a showing given for Deco Martinez, the ex-gang member turned artist. But Valdar brought some people with him that I didn't care to associate with."

"Because...?"

"They were Russian, like Valdar. He was very friendly to Martinez, but Valdar's little group discouraged any intruders into their clic, except for Robert Landman, the actor, and Frank Meadows and his wife. They were well received. Everyone else was given cold stares and silence."

"No other artists got close?"

"Only Deco."

We talked another ten minutes without anything making me jump up and shout "Eureka!", so I thanked Harold and left. By the time I reached our office, the sun was backlighting low clouds on the horizon like a halo. Hondo sat at his desk eating half a Subway's sandwich. The other half was on my desk, along with a canned Coca-Cola Classic.

"It was good of you to cook," I said.

"I figured you'll need your strength. Bond called a couple minutes ago, said she was at your house and had a surprise waiting for you."

I looked at the sandwich, "Maybe I shouldn't eat, then. Maybe she cooked."

"I don't think you want to wait."

Something was making the hairs on my arms stand up. "What is it?"

"There was a message left on the answering machine when I got here about a minute before Bond called. I didn't listen to it until after she hung up. The message was from Hunter. She got an earlier flight out and called on her cell phone to say that she was on her way to your house, since she didn't know where my new house or our new office was. She also said she had a surprise for you."

I wondered if I could disappear across the border, maybe live in a fishing village in Baja under an assumed name.

Hondo said, "You need to get over there in case they get testy."

"Come on with me."

"All right." He stood up and pointed at my sandwich, "You going to eat that?"

"I've lost my appetite."

**

We went in Hondo's Mercedes and I was torn between wanting him to hurry and wanting us never to get there. I was not looking forward to this one. We reached the house and saw the front door standing wide open. Bond's Jaguar was the only car in the driveway.

I went to the door and looked at the living room. Nothing was broken, and there were no bullet holes in anything I could see. I stepped in and Bond came out of the bedroom wearing shorts and a tee shirt. She saw us, walked over and kissed me. Her mouth tasted of ice and orange slices and bourbon. She pulled back and looked at me when I didn't respond.

Bond said, "I had a visitor a bit ago. Gave me quite a start. She evidently has a key because I'd locked the door before I went into the bedroom to prepare a special surprise for you."

I felt my shoulders sag and a deep heaviness sink into the center of me.

Bond continued, "We had an intense discussion for a while, then she left."

"Did she say anything?"

"Oh, she said lots of things, but if you mean when she left, yes. She said she would talk to Hondo tomorrow."

Hondo said, "I'll come by in the morning, pick you up." He left without saying good-bye to Bond.

I went to the couch and Bond sat beside me, playing with the hairs on my neck. She said, "Don't you want to go into the bedroom, let me show you my surprise?"

I was silent for a minute, then said, "No, I'm not up to it tonight."

She got upset. "Just what is your problem? Do you have the hots for her? If that's the case, then fine, bring her back and we can all three enjoy each other. It might liven up what's turning out to be a real shit of an evening."

"I think it might be best if you leave."

Bond jerked to her feet and said, "Fine! You don't know what you're giving up, *Mr.* Baca." She stormed into the bedroom and came out carrying a small overnight bag. "And you can consider yourself fired, too. You're off the case, you asshole!" She went out the open door and I heard the Jaguar start and wheels squeal as she left.

I leaned forward and rested my head in my hands. No matter what my intentions, I have a way of screwing up with women without even trying. I walked to the door and closed it, then went to the cabinet to take out a bottle and try to kill enough brain cells so that I'd get rid of the ones that carried the memory of this night.

**

I woke the next morning at sunrise with a good one. The Flintstones glass was still half-full of orange juice and vodka, the ice long melted, and I had a throbber of a headache that started behind my right eye and ran back along my skull and down my neck, which felt like it was impaled with ice picks. My tongue felt coated and I could smell my own breath. I walked to the kitchen and drank two large glasses of water, then went to the bedroom and put on my gym shorts, running shoes and a white tee shirt and went out the door.

The first mile was probably equal to the death march on Bataan. In the first four hundred yards, I struggled, with my calves and thighs aching like a bad tooth. I huffed and croaked, gasping as I tried to pull in enough air through lungs that felt as small as soda straws. The sweat started early and my shirt was soaked at the end of the first five minutes. I kept at it. At the end of the second mile, I thought I might live. I continued for a third before slowing to an easy walk and circling back to the house. I was okay physically when I got there, and I showered, changed, drank coffee, and ate toast while I waited for Hondo.

He drove up at seven-thirty and we headed to the office.
He said, "How are you feeling?"
"Okay."
"I talked to Hunter last night after I got home. She stayed in a hotel last night, but I talked her into coming over to talk."
"I didn't plan for that to happen."
"I told her that, but I couldn't tell her you and Bond weren't sleeping together. Seems Bond put the knife in and twisted it while she and Hunter were talking, made it out that you and she were long time lovers, that she'd been living with you for months. You can sure pick them."
"Can't I. By the way, Bond fired us last night after you left."
"You told her to leave, didn't you?"
"Uh-huh. That was her parting shot."
Hondo let a big smile spread across his face.
I said, "What are you smiling about?"
"We get to send her money back and don't have to be tied to her anymore."
"Yeah, but we *do* have to eat, pay bills, stuff like that."

"I've still got a few dollars in the bank, and we don't have car payments – well, we've got to pay for Shamu's body work, and we can wash towels and clean up for Archie in the gym to take care of rent. We're on top of the world."

"What about food?"

"I've got three bags of Julio's chips and three jars of salsa that Hunter brought. They're in the trunk. Between that and the large box of uncooked spaghetti in my cabinet, we can live large."

"These the chips we were getting for Vick?"

"He'll never know."

Everything else was going to hell, so I said, "Why not?"

To celebrate our new independence we took the bags of chips and jars of salsa into the office. We opened one bag and one jar and ate them while we talked. Both of us had a mouthful when the phone rang.

I pushed the speaker button so we could both hear and said around the food, "Heawoe."

"Baca, is that you?" It was Sergeant Vick Best.

I chewed faster and swallowed, "Hello, Vick. How you doing?"

He was silent a moment before saying, "You eating something? Say, those better not be my chips!"

"Vick, it's nine o'clock in the morning. What in the world would we be doing eating your chips at this time of day? I mean, jeez, think about it." Hondo scooped what looked like a half-cup of salsa on one chip and raised it to his mouth.

Vick said, "Hondo, you'd tell me if Ronny was eating my chips, right?"

Hondo stopped the chip an inch from his mouth and said, "I'm looking at him right now, and there's not a thing in his mouth." He opened wide, put the chip in his mouth and smiled as he chewed.

"All right then. What I called for, the crime scene team finished up at Landman's Malibu home. Now, I know you two said you weren't there and I'm not gonna push it, but I thought you might want to know what we found."

I sat a little straighter, "Yeah, Vick, we would."

Vick said, "There were blood types from three people, so it was quite a fight. We also found the top part of an ear that had been bitten off."

"Is Mike Tyson a suspect?"

"Very funny. The ear was from a white guy. We also found some long hair that had been pulled out of someone's head."

"The roots come with it?"

"Yeah, male, O positive."

"The ear and the hair from the same guy?"

"Nope, two different people."

"What color was it?"

"What, the hair?"

"Yeah."

"Blond."

"Blond-blonde, or some other kind of blond?"

"If you know something, Baca, you'd better tell me."

"I just want to help, Officer Vick. If I run into some blonde with a chunk of hair missing, I want to be clear on whether to call you or not."

"It's sort of dishwater blond, like that. Hell, I'm not a beautician." We could hear somebody in the background talking to him. He said, "I have to go. There's another meeting with the press. Got the Mayor and the Governor both here with me on this one."

"Your right profile's your best. It's very Clint Eastwood. Keep it toward the camera."

"Yeah, funny guy. Just you and Hondo be careful. We've got two missing persons now, and lots of blood around. I don't want you going into anything with your eyes closed."

"Thanks, Vick."

"Get me my chips."

"We're on it. I tell you, they're so close I can taste them."

"Asshole." He hung up.

Hondo rolled the top of the bag to close it and said, "That's enough. We need to save some for Hunter, she brought them."

My insides fluttered. "When's she coming?"

"Any minute."

"My hands are clammy."

"Dig into your *chi*. Chant one of those sayings you always tell me, like, '*What is the sound of one hand clapping*', one of those."

I didn't have a chance to reply because Hunter opened the door. I hadn't seen her in over a year but she still looked great. I felt a jumble of confused feelings: guilt, sorrow, joy, affection, and yes, love, but the way one loves a lifelong friend. Well, maybe a little lust, too, because she was so good looking.

Hunter walked over, sat in the chair by Hondo's desk, and turned it to face me. "Hondo and I talked a lot last night. You're lucky to have such a good friend."

"Yes, I am."

I started to say more but she held up her hand, "Let me say this, then we'll see where things stand." I nodded and Hunter continued, "I don't know what to feel. I was ready last night to get back with you, be with you from now on." She leaned forward, put her elbows on her knees, and looked at the floor as she clasped her hands together. She raised her head and looked at me, "When that Meadows woman started laying it on last night about you and her, well, my self confidence has never been very high when it comes to me being able to keep a relationship. I bought everything she said, and she was good, going into detail about how she pleased you, doing this and that," I started to speak but she held up her hand again, "Let me finish. So she convinced me, and adding that to the surprise of finding her in your home, well it was too much. I left and called Hondo later. I was ready to book a flight back to El Paso when he talked me into coming to his house."

She sat up in the chair and looked at both of us. She said to me, "You know what the first thing was he said to me?"

I shook my head because my throat was too constricted to talk.

"He said, 'Quit trying to convince yourself you want Ronny as a lover. It makes it too hard on all of us.' I sputtered and cried and fumed and stomped around, and Hondo let me. He let me get it all out. We talked a lot after that, and I thought more about it after I left him. And here's what I think." She got up from the chair and went to Hondo, held his face and kissed him on the lips, then came to me and did the same. When she sat back down she said, "I love you both, as friends, the way it should be for us. Ronny, you and I never, ever should have gotten involved. Man, that was doomed from the get-go."

Hondo said, "What she told me last night was you were an idiot around beautiful women."

Hunter interrupted him and said, "I meant you had strong desires and weak control in that area."

Hondo said, "I told her you stayed as horny as a forty-balled tiger."

Hunter nodded, "Yeah, that's what Mr. Eloquence said. But the point is, that's my problem to deal with, and for all the years before we got involved, I was fine with it. It was only after I brainwashed myself that you and I were meant to be together that it became a big deal."

I said, "You're not wrong, we were meant to be together."

Hondo said, "Yep, we were."

Hunter said, "The three of us. Maybe so. Just give me some time to work on it. Now, you have anything to eat?"

Hondo reached for the bag of chips, "I've got just the thing."

CHAPTER SIX

While we ate the rest of the bag, we filled Hunter in on the case. She was particularly interested in Carl Rakes.

"His tattoos, were they bright?"

"I guess you'd call them that. They were dark ink, but showed real well, shiny, no fading anywhere."

"Those are Russian prison tattoos. They make the ink from shoe soles and urine."

"What?"

"Yeah, they take a shoe sole and burn it until it all turns into soot, then sift it through a handkerchief until it's a very fine dust, then they mix urine with it. They prefer to use the urine of the person they're going to work on."

"How the heck do you know that?"

"The case I worked on in Florida, we had some guys with tattoos and we asked about them through the interpreter. Found out what some of the symbols and phrases meant, too. Skulls mean people they have murdered or killed in fights, a pirate means robbery. American money indicates they're with the new order of Russian gangster, and those people are as smart and vicious as they come. They're after quick money any way they can get it, and they take out anyone in their way. They're good at money laundering, too."

"So you think Rakes is Russian Mafia?"

"No doubt in my mind."

Hondo said, "Makes you wonder what he's doing with Meadows."

I said, "Why don't we drive down to Siberia and see if they're there? It wouldn't hurt to look them over a little closer now that we have our expert with us."

Hondo pointed at the clock that read 11:00AM and said, "Let's grab an early lunch first. I need something besides chips to take me through the rest of the day."

As we got up to leave I moved beside Hunter and said, "You know, you being the Soviet expert and all, I've heard that Russian women have this technique they do with their tongues-"

Hunter elbowed me so hard in the ribs a speedloader popped loose.

**

Siberia was busy when we entered. There were probably a hundred customers scattered around the room and the vents were barely keeping up with the cloud of cigarette and cigar smoke that hung against the ceiling in a layer a foot thick. Frank Meadows was holding court in the same place as before, and Carl Rakes was coming from the bar with two drinks, neither of which was a Tunguska Blast. The wuss. Rakes wore a skintight white tee shirt and his tattoos showed through like cloud shadow. He walked in front of us and I noticed he still had the meat tenderizer mark on his forehead.

As he passed, Hondo said, "Hey, Wafflehead."

Rakes stopped, turned and recognized Hondo, then me, "You tink id is over? My turn vill come, and I ged you, your friend, then take my time with your pretty girl here." He looked Hunter up and down and ran his tongue across his lips like he was tasting something.

"We can dance anytime you want," Hunter said. She was beautiful and feminine, with a healthy dose of tomboy, and people tended to underestimate her. Hunter had been in several gunfights down on the border and was a three-time State Champ in Combat Pistol. Carl had better be careful wishing for that.

Frank Meadows came over and took one of the drinks from Rakes. He said, "The fuck you doing here, Baca? My wife fired you, remember?"

"You're absolutely right, Frankie, I don't work for her anymore. Funny how you know Bond fired me. She went through a lot of trouble telling me she was scared you would find out. That's a pretty good bullshit game you two play. But then again, she's a good actor. You know, Frankie Boy, maybe you should use her in some of your flops."

"You want something, or you come down to run your mouth?"

"We came down to go slumming."

Frank was an ass, but he wasn't dumb. "Just stay out of my way, understand? I conduct business here and if you cost me a multi-million dollar deal, there'll be more mad people banging on your door than you can count."

Hondo said, "He can count pretty high."

I noticed several men in the crowd work their way nearer to us. They had that tough look, but were acting uninterested in our little group. I said, "Nice talking to you Frank, it always makes me appreciate breathing outside air after we've been close." I motioned to Hunter and Hondo and we turned to leave, but not before we saw Rakes toast us with his glass, bite a chunk out of it and grin as he chewed.

**

As we turned onto Sunset, Hunter said, "There were quite a few Russians in there, lots of tats."

"I thought that might be it," I said. "Kind of a base of operations."

"That would be my guess. Did you notice the small tats on the side of Rakes' neck?"

Hondo said, "Yeah, looked like a couple of crooked knifes or something side by side."

"That's a sign he's an enforcer and one of their higher-ups, a lieutenant, something like that. He's camouflaged real well, acting like he's working class, even if it is for this Meadows guy."

"What you're telling us is that he's a boss of others."

"Oh yeah."

We thought on that as we drove to make our appointment with Loomis at the Camino Real Motel.

Loomis was expecting us when we walked into the lobby. He held up a paper and shoved it at me when we reached the counter. "Here, I told you he signed it."

I looked at the photocopy of the sign-in paper and sure enough, Robert Landman had signed in a flowing script. I looked at the rest of it and it showed Number of Occupants as four.

"He had four people with him?"

"More than that. Must've been eight or ten when they all finally got here."

Hondo said, "You remember anything about them, what they looked like?"

"They were different kinds. The man and woman who came in with him, then some hard, blocky looking men and two Mexican women, good looking, too. Had kinda strawberry colored hair, like that. There was a big-shouldered Mexican, came in, too. He's the one who left with the two Mexican women. Lucky guy."

"Did they all come in together?"

"No, the man and woman came with Landman, then the group of white guys with the two Mexican women, and the big Mexican came in solo. Hey, it wasn't like they were crowded up there. That one is our premiere suite, really two rooms made into one big one. There are tables and a bar and three beds and fold out sofas, the works. You could probably keep twenty people there, no problem-o."

"You rent that out often?"

"No, in fact nobody's rented it since he did."

"You think we could go up for a look?"

Loomis looked around, "I don't know..."

I laid out another hundred-dollar bill.

He put it in his pocket and said, "Okay, I guess so. Don't stay long, though. My manager comes back at two." He slid the key to me and said, "It's on the second floor, all the way to the end."

We entered the room and each of us took a different area. The maids had done a good job and the place smelled clean, the beds made without a wrinkle, and there was no trash left anywhere. Hondo checked the refrigerator and found nothing. I went into the bathroom and went through all the drawers. On a hunch, I lifted the lid off the toilet reservoir. Clear water and a few rust stains were along the sides, and nothing was in the bottom. As I started to put the lid on, I heard the faint sound of water leaking. I looked closer in the tank and saw a black thread tied to the flapper and going underneath it. I flushed the toilet and held the ball up. A string hung into the opening. When the water finished running, I held up the float and pulled on the string. At the end was a small baggie rolled like a loose cigarette. Papers were inside. I untied the string and took the baggie into the kitchen.

Hondo and Hunter came over as I opened it and spread out the papers. They were in Spanish and Hunter looked them over and translated.

"These are papers of a woman from Durango named Maria Sanchez de Mendoza. There's also a note she wrote that says if something happens to her, to notify her mother. It gives the address. Her last sentence says she is scared but hopeful, that these people are very dangerous, but that her older sister said she can make lots of money in the club. She says, and I'm quoting here, 'The star is protecting us for now.' Then there's a 'Thanks to God' and that's it." Hunter looked at me.

I said, "I wonder what club, and how this ties in with Landman? Is he dangerous? Man, I can't see that."

Hondo said, "I think star means Landman."

Hunter said, "If that's true, then he's not dangerous, he's in danger."

"Or worse," I said.

We returned to the lobby and Loomis asked, "You find anything?"

"Nah, but thanks for letting us look around."

"Sure thing," he leaned closer and with his crossed eyes, I couldn't tell if he was looking at Hondo or me when he said, "Anything coming up good in the rag I should keep an eye out for?"

I got some control and said, "You bet, I don't know what date yet, but you read it for the next couple months and you'll see what I'm talking about." I winked at him.

Loomis grinned and winked back, his face pointed somewhere between Hondo and me. "All right!"

Hondo said, "If any of those people show up, you give us a call."

He handed Loomis a card and he read it, then frowned, "Private Investigators? I thought you were with the Enquirer."

"It's a cover," Hondo said.

Loomis nodded as he thought about it, then grinned and nodded harder. "I get it." He looked at me and said, "You got a card?" I gave him my card. He read it and frowned again, "Baca? You don't look like these gangbangers around here."

I pointed at Hondo and Hunter and said, "My brother and sister and I were orphans in Bolognia, you know, over in Europe, close to Mayonasia."

Loomis nodded and said, "Yeah, I think I saw something about it on CNN."

"You probably did," I said. "We all were adopted by different families over here."

"So your names are different. Makes sense. I knew you weren't really Mexican."

I nodded and said, "You got it."

We left, with Hunter whispering, "God-o-mighty."

**

At the office, we opened a bag of Julio's and a jar of salsa and put it on Hondo's desk. We talked about things between bites.

Hunter said, "I'm going to make a few calls, see if I can run down the mother in Durango. From the address, she doesn't have a phone so I'll need to get somebody to find the colonia she lives in; get them to help her call me."

I said, "What about the club? Is it even in Los Angeles? How are we going to narrow that down?"

"The journey begins with a single step." Hondo held up his fingers in a V and said, "Peace, my brother."

I rolled my eyes. "You weren't even *born* in the sixties."

Hondo said, "The sixties are a state of mind." Hunter leaned back in her chair to watch us.

I said, "Aren't you the one who told me last month that people back then were too innocent?"

"They've been having Sixties week on the History Channel. Some pretty good stuff. Makes you appreciate events back then a little better."

"Good grief."

"They talked a lot about the Soviet Union, and later, on Court TV they had a special on the Russian Mafia."

That Hondo, sometimes he had a way of getting to the point that defied all logic. I said, "So, you're making a statement here?"

"Sure. The first step's got to be from where we are now."

I thought a moment and said, "So, where we are is...?"

Hondo looked at me as if he was a teacher and I was a third grader who just missed two plus two.

"What?" I said.

He made a small sigh, "We have Bond and Frank Meadows, Carl Rakes the ex-convict who's probably served time in a Russian prison, then Bob Landman and a painter from the Volga. Then there are undocumented Mexican women — strawberry blonde Mexican women, Landman's yellow bike, and *anothe*r strawberry blond Mexican woman in the Camino Real. All with Landman and a bunch of others that sound like Rakes and some Mexican bad boys. We find a note about danger and clubs and finally, Loomis telling us what he saw."

I thought of Loomis also telling us about Elvis, but didn't interrupt.

Hunter dipped some salsa with a chip and ate as she thought. She let her chair down and said, "Yeah, I think I see where you're going."

Going? I started to argue, and then something clicked. "Russians, Siberia on Sunset. If they're tied to the Mafia and have one club in Los Angeles, then they've got others."

Hunter said, "The way they launder money in Florida, is mixing it with legitimate income from strip bars and gentlemen's clubs, all the places where women dance nude. They control it all, from picking the women to picking the toilet paper."

I said, "We check out the probable ones, see if we find some blond Mexican women working there and we've got a connection, which might lead us to Landman."

Hondo nodded, "That's what I said." He glanced across the office at the door and quickly placed the chips and salsa under his desk.

I started to say something when Sergeant Vick Best opened the door and walked in.

"Baca, where's that sperm whale pickup of yours? It is not in the lot. I wasn't sure you were here."

I said, "It's not a sperm whale, it's...never mind. My *pickup* is in the shop, getting some body work done."

He moved his head back and forth, sniffing the air as he said, "What happened, they have to Bond-O all the harpoon marks? Hey, do I smell some chips?"

Hondo reached into his desk and pulled out the last unopened bag of Julio's. Hunter got the remaining jar of salsa out of the small refrigerator and placed it beside the chips.

"Thank you, young lady."

She shook his hand and said, "A pleasure, Sergeant. My name's Hunter Kincaid. I've heard a lot about you from Ronny and Hondo."

"Well, you be careful around these two. They tend to get friends into situations." He rubbed at a point over his left hip as he talked.

Hondo said, "That old bullet wound acting up, Sergeant? I didn't think a twenty-two would take that long to heal."

Vick looked hard at me, "Yeah well, sometimes it acts up when it's irritated.

Vick was getting all stirred up and agitated and I could hear the chips breaking in the sack under his arm. I said, "What brings you down, or do you just like our company?"

"They found a small shark this morning washed up on Malibu. Some tourist opened its mouth and saw a foot wedged in there."

I said, "Shark? You sure it wasn't sole?"

Vick half closed his eyes like he had a headache, "You are hopeless, you know that? What it is, they think it might be from Valdar because forensics found small flakes of paint on it. I thought if you knew that, you might stop snooping around and getting into trouble." He was squeezing the bag of chips under his arm again.

Hunter stood up and took them from him, "Let me carry these to the car for you, Sergeant. We'll walk down together and get acquainted."

"Thank you, Miss." Before Vick left, he walked over to me and leaned down to whisper, "You still owe me two bags of chips and two jars of salsa, don't think I didn't notice."

Hunter stayed outside with him for ten minutes before returning. When she returned, she shook her head at the empty bag of chips on Hondo's desk. "He's a nice man. He likes you two a lot, but doesn't want you to know."

Hondo said, "You were out there a while. What'd you find out?"

"I thought it might narrow down the search if I quizzed him about Russian crime in LA. He's aware of the East European organizations moving in, works with an FBI task force that's looking into the spread of the Russian Mafia in California and their partnerships with other criminal families. What Vick said, there are several factions working in Los Angeles, each bumping against the other for bigger pieces of the pie."

"He mention anything about Siberia?"

"Yeah, I didn't even have to prime him. He was telling me they've looked at several companies that run bars around the county, and he mentioned five or six names, but one is called the Sarana Corporation and it owns a piece of Siberia and a dozen or so other strip clubs scattered around town."

Hondo said, "That'll help. I'll go down to the county and city offices, check the abstracts and talk to a couple of people, see what I can find on Sarana."

Hunter said, "I'll go with you. I can make my calls on the cell, and two people looking will go faster."

Hondo said to me, "How about you?"

"I'll make some calls, go check out a couple hunches," I didn't want to say in front of Hunter that I was heading straight to the strip bars. My ribs were still bruised from her last shot.

When they were gone I pulled out the yellow pages and looked through the Nightclubs section for some ideas, got one that looked promising and went next door to borrow Archie's Corvette.

The Caspian Diamond Gentlemen's Club was in West Hollywood in the center of the large Russian community. Thirty or so cars were in the lot when I arrived. I parked the Corvette and went to the smoked glass doors where a large, polite man in a dark suit and long blond ponytail opened the door to let me enter.

The inside looked as black as a cave after being in the sun, and it took my eyes a few seconds to adjust. There was a central stage with a dancing pole and two smaller stages and poles in two corners. In between them were round tables, chairs, and a circle of stools surrounding the dancing platforms. The half-circle bar took up the far wall and the shape allowed customers to swivel and see the shows without too much trouble.

There was one g-stringed dancer on center stage doing a good number with the pole as Pink sang through the speakers. I sat down at a table against the wall so I could see the entire room. I ordered a beer from the waitress and watched the dancer some more. She hung upside down on the shiny pole using only her wrapped legs to grip as her arms waved free in snaky movements. Her head was five feet off the floor and she controlled her slide down the pole with her thigh muscles. My mind started wondering what a woman who could do that with her thighs would be able to do in...I tried to clear my thoughts and check out the customers.

Most were early-offs from work, but I recognized three of the ones at the bar as three who had been playing pool in Siberia when I had my little run-in with Frank Meadows and Carl Rakes.

They wore jackets, and it wasn't cold in here or outside. I figured that since I was wearing a jacket and had a gun, then everybody in this place who had on a jacket was probably heeled, too. I checked out the other patrons and there were only four jackets in the entire place, and I was one of them.

I didn't know if they had recognized me or not, but I was careful not to make any moves and attract attention. I sat there for a half hour and saw several patrons leave and a few others come in. The three men at the bar didn't move. I ordered two more beers and downed them at ten dollars a pop. Right when I was rising to leave, another dancer came out. Enrique Iglesias sang through the speakers about wanting to be my hero as a strawberry blond Mexican woman danced toward the pole. She looked like one of the women we'd seen in the canyon. She was naked, not wearing a stitch and her tiny body was tight and taut. I watched her routine and when the song was almost over, I walked to the steps leading off the stage. When she came down, I could see I'd been wrong, that she wasn't one of the women at the canyon but an older version of them, someone in their thirties.

As she smiled at me and stepped down to pass I said, "You're from Durango, right?"

Her smiled faltered a moment then caught again and she said in perfect English, "No, I'm from here. But I'll give you this, that's the oddest come-on line I've ever heard."

"I apologize. You looked like someone I know from there."

"Well, I'm sorry to disappoint you. Maybe I can cheer you up with my next dance."

A drunk staggered to us and spilled part of his full beer on my pants as he looked with adoration at the woman. He wore a pale blue uniform shirt with *Calvin* embroidered over the pocket. He held a five-dollar bill toward the woman and tried to push me out of the way, "Thass my woman, buddy, thass the woman I love."

I went with his push and he fell like he'd leaned against a door and missed. The glass tinked and clunked on the floor and sprayed beer across the feet of two men coming out of an office door.

One of them was a tall, very lean man with a slim, silver-headed cane. He wore a black Armani suit that matched the wet-looking, combed-back black hair. The hair fit his skull like a helmet.

The other man was Carl Rakes.

The small woman stepped back as Carl jerked Calvin off the floor with one hand and slammed him against the wall. Calvin's feet fluttered six inches off the floor as if he was walking on air.

Carl said, "You hairshid piece of horseneck face!"

I snorted and Carl pointed to me with his free hand, "And you, I nod forget you, Baca."

I spoke to the other man, "You want to rein in your puppy? This poor guy was drunk, that's all."

He stepped to within three feet of me and held the slender cane across his thighs in a relaxed pose. The right hand stayed on the silver handle. He wasn't just lean; he was thin to emaciation, with a gaunt face, hollow cheeks and eyes as black as a vampire's. His deep voice had an east European accent as he said, "I do not tell Carl what to do. He will do as he pleases."

"Bella Lugosi," I said.

He frowned, "What?"

"You know, Dracula, from the old black and white movie they show on late night TV. You're trying to sound like Lugosi. Try this," I did my best Dracula imitation, "Listen to them, the Children of the Night, Blahh."

He took it in for a moment, then the smallest smile appeared. It looked like a death rictus. "Carl, let the customer go." Carl started to say something but the dark haired man spoke in a foreign language and Carl dropped Calvin like a piece of dirty laundry. Calvin scuttled off on his hands and knees like a crab and disappeared into the darkness between the tables. The man said to me, "It will be best if you go, too. Carl doesn't always do as I request."

I stuck out my hand and said, "I hate to leave without introductions. My name's Ronny Baca and you are...?"

He didn't take my hand, but said, "Simon Mortay. Leave."

I took his advice, but as I left, I saw Carl grab the strawberry-haired woman by the arm and jerk her into the office. Simon Mortay, Old Mister Creepy watched me until I went out the door.

There was a place in the back edge of the parking lot where I could see both doors, so I pulled the Corvette into place and settled into the seat.

Four hours later when the sun was setting, I decided I had to leave and find a place to pee. Those three beers I'd had were knocking on my bladder door and demanding to be let out. As I started the car and pulled away, the club's back door opened and the strawberry-haired woman walked across the lot.

So much for relief. I turned the wheel and followed her to a green Lexus. She recognized me as I got out, "Mister, you crazy? They got video on this lot, and if Carl or Mr. Mortay see you...They don't play by the rules, you understand?"

"Okay, get in and come with me, we'll go someplace safer."

"Don't you get it? I don't want them to see me with you."

"Did they hurt you after I left? I saw Carl grab you, take you into the office."

"Look, I don't like to see people hurt. You gotta go."

"One last question." And it really was the last question unless I didn't mind wetting myself in public.

She rolled her eyes and sighed, "What?"

"I thought Carl Rakes worked for Frank Meadows. What's he doing with Mortay?"

She shook her head and got in the Lexus. Before she closed the door she said, "You don't know shit, do you?" She drove off before I could say, No, I don't. I got into the Corvette, which because of my bladder being the size of a weather balloon, felt small and uncomfortable. I drove as fast as I dared until a Mickey D's sign appeared and I slid into a parking place and trotted inside. When I finally got to the urinal, it was such a relief my eyes watered. I sighed when I finished, then went to the sink and was about to wash my hands when the door opened and the three jacket-wearing men I'd seen at The Caspian Diamond walked in and stood behind me. There was no one else in the bathroom. One of the men leaned his back against the door.

I filled one hand with the pink liquid pump soap as I looked at them in the mirror and said, "I'm not who you think I am, I'm his twin brother.

The biggest one said, "Ve know you, Baca. Is nod to fool us vith your talk smart mouth."

I angled myself at a forty-five to them, the soap cupped in my left hand. "Okay, Boris, what were you told to tell me?"

"I am not Boris, and we were to tell you nothing."

"Well okay then, I guess I'll be going. You three have a gay old time here in the bathroom." I looked at Not Boris and said, "That's a joke, get it?"

"We have a joke, too. Our joke is to beat you."

I figured that meant talk was over.

I shot my left hand to Not Boris' eyes, jabbing my fingers and the soap deep in them. He yelled and put his hands to his face as he fell back. I pivoted as he fell and sent a side-kick to the throat of the second one. He backpedaled into a stall, holding his neck as his eyes bulged out. The third one came off the door a little slow and reached under his jacket. I hit him a solid shot over the heart with the heel of my right palm. He made a croak and dropped to his knees. I punched down at his jaw, laying him face down on the tile.

I reached under his jacket and pulled out a Beretta, then went to the other two and did the same. I stuck the guns in my waistband and caught a glimpse of myself in the mirror. Like William Holden heading for the last shootout in The Wild Bunch. I went to Not Boris, who was trying to get water out of a toilet bowl to clean his eyes.

"Just thought I'd tell you," I said, "That's used water you're putting on your face. Somebody forgot to flush."

He felt around and found the flush handle, pushed it and said to me without looking up, "I ged you for this."

My nerves were still jangling and that pissed me off, so I snap-kicked the back of his head hard enough to drive his nose into the edge of the toilet. Bright crimson drops pattered the water like a leaky faucet, each one leaving a tiny pink octopus with tendril arms floating on the surface. Not Boris raised his head and pinched the nose shut with a thumb and forefinger.

I said, "You tell Mortay any more of this and I'm coming for him. I won't be playing, either."

Not Boris said, "Mortay did not send us."

That stopped me. "Okay, who did?"

He shook his head and said, "You know nothing, Baca."

I was getting tired of everyone telling me that. "You don't work for Simon Mortay?"

He shook his head, "Stupid, stupid man."

"You want me to kick you again? Tell me who sent you."

I could hear the others stirring behind me.

He wouldn't talk, but smiled at me with pink teeth and terrible bloodshot eyes. I waited as long as I could, then I left before all three were back on their feet and I had to shoot somebody.

I gunned the Corvette and was on the road in seconds, squirming all the way as the pistols dug into me like sharp sticks.

CHAPTER SEVEN

I was waiting at the office when Hondo and Hunter came back. Hunter went to a chair and sat down, saying, "I aged ten years today."

Hondo was carrying a bag of Julio's and a jar of salsa.

I sat up, looking from Hunter to Hondo. "Where'd you get that?"

Hondo said, "We were at the courthouse, and when we came out, the Mayor, the Governor and our own Sergeant Vick Best were holding a press conference at the front of the building. Hunter and I went around the edge of the crowd and happened to walk by the Sergeant's personal vehicle."

"How'd you know it was his?"

Hondo said, "Remember the barbeque you threw for him last year, where he backed his Bronco into that orange Chevy?"

"Yeah, I told him the orange in the dent made it look like a Hook-'Em Horns brand."

Well, he never got it fixed, so the orange still shows in the dent, and it still looks the same."

"What's that got to do with the chips?"

"I saw them in the front seat and took them."

I rubbed my forehead, "You broke into a Deputy Sheriff's car?"

"It's not like we aren't friends."

"Wasn't it locked?"

"That's a relative term."

Hunter said, "He picked the lock before I even knew what he was doing. He said, 'Hey, look, there are Vick's chips,' and then he squatted down and pulled me with him and had the door open before I had time to wet my pants."

"Wasn't the alarm set?"

"Heck yes. It was wailing away when he snatched the stuff. He handed it to me and closed the door. Did it so fast it was like the door never opened. Then he told me, 'How about some double-time duck walking,' and he banged on a half dozen cars as we went, setting off their alarms, too."

Hondo said, "Caused a little delay in the speech as people went to their cars and zapped them with the alarm buttons on their key chains. No big deal, they always blame it on kids, anyhow."

I felt a headache coming on. "Are you going to eat them?"

"We could, I guess. What I thought is give them to Vick, that way you'll only owe him one more bag and jar of salsa."

"But it's the same bag."

"Not to him it isn't."

"You may have a point there."

Hunter said, "You two are going to be the death of me."

We put the chips and salsa away and Hunter said, "I contacted an investigator friend of mine at Immigration and he's working on getting the woman in Durango to call me. He said he'll call me and let me know when to expect her."

"Is she going to call you on your cell?"

"Seemed like the best way."

I nodded. "Any time frame?"

"He thought maybe today, for sure tomorrow. A friend of his works out of the Juarez office and is in Durango this week, not far from where the woman lives."

"That would be good."

Hondo said, "You should have heard Hunter talking to him, all sweet and saying 'Doll' this and 'Sweetheart' that."

I felt a little prickle, "You got something going with this guy?"

"Don't you even start, Ronny Baca." She leaned over and whacked Hondo on the shoulder, "And you, Mr. Troublemaker, quit taking my words out of context." Hondo rubbed his shoulder and grinned.

Old Hondo. Ha-ha. I asked him, "You find out anything?"

Hondo said, "The Sarana Corporation is partner in twenty-two pieces of property in the LA area, everything from buildings to warehouses to vacant lots."

"Who owns Sarana?"

"Other corporations, about a dozen of them, and those corporations are, in turn, owned by other corporations. We didn't have time to run out the trail to a person's name."

"So they're covers."

"Can't be anything else."

"You copy down the lists of the properties?"

He gave me a paper and said, "Hunter and I have copies, too." As I looked over the list, I saw The Caspian Diamond listed. Hondo said, "How about you, you do any good?"

I told them what happened, and for a few minutes, we discussed how it all fit together, then decided we needed some Chinese for brain food. I volunteered to go and slipped on my Patagonia. I was two steps from the office door when it opened and Mickey flew in and hugged me tight, her face going like a magnet to my jacket as she bawled her head off and said in quivering, muffled sobs, "She-she fired me, she fired me."

"Who?"

"Bond."

"That's Landman's office."

"Sh-she ran me off, told me I had no more business in Bob's office or his life or on the studio lot." Mickey hawed and rolled her head back and forth on my chest.

I patted her back and said, "Hey, we got fired, too. Don't worry."

She looked up at me and I felt my eyebrows rise. I hadn't seen but a blur of Mickey's face when she ran in, and this was the first real look. Frankenstein would have been proud. Mickey had used some sort of pea green eye shadow and overdone clumpy mascara that mixed with all those tears to form a gloppy paste that obscured one eyebrow and coated half her forehead and one ear. Yummy.

She said, "You're fired, too?" I nodded and she wailed again, "Oh noooo! Now Bob's got no one to help him."

"Mickey, we got fired, but we haven't stopped looking."

"Y-you haven't? You're going to find Bob even when you're not being paid?"

"Uh-huh. Just makes it easier since we don't have any Meadows people telling us what to do."

Mickey hugged me harder and said, "You are so *noble*. Like a chivalrous knight from the old days." That got an eye roll from Hunter. Mickey sniffled and pulled back. I handed her my handkerchief and she dabbed at her eyes and touched her hair, aware for the first time of Hunter in the room. "I'm sorry, I must look a mess." I pointed to the bathroom and she disappeared behind the door.

Hunter said, "You as Sir Galahad," she shook her head, "God-o-mighty."

Hondo said, "That windbreaker will be so threadbare after another cleaning you'll be able to see through it."

I took it off, careful to keep my fingers out of the wet spots and dropped it on the floor by my desk.

When Mickey came out, her eyes were red and puffy and she looked a little pale. She said, "I'm glad you're still on the case. If you don't find Bob, no one can."

I said, "Tell me what happened."

"Well, I was at my desk and was through with everything I could do, so I went into Bob's office and looked around for anything that might help us. There wasn't anything startling, the last thing he made notes on was the need for preparation for Ninety Notches."

Hunter looked at Hondo, who said, "A Border Patrol movie that's in the works."

Mickey said, "Bob made several notes about immersing himself in the role, of getting the feel of what it's like."

Hondo said, "Like the picture we found, the one Valdar was painting."

"Sort of, but more intense, more thorough. Bob told me many times that he has to live in the role before playing it. Like once, when he was to portray a small town police officer, he used an alias and some faked papers to get a job as a real policeman in some town in New Mexico and worked there for two months. He arrested people, gave out tickets, broke up fights, everything a real cop would do. The studio almost had a stroke when they found out. That's the kind of thing he does to prepare."

I said, "So, to portray a Border Patrol Agent, what would he do?"

We were all silent, thinking it through when Hunter said, "He'd do it in stages."

"Like what?" I said.

"He'd start with the uniform, the gear, then get a feel for working outdoors."

Hondo said, "Yeah, then he'd read up on things—hey Mickey, in the script, what would he have been trying to do?"

"The bad guys were some smugglers, a gang of them and he was going after them."

"Uh-huh. Bob would get some angles on smuggling, do some reading on it and see what was happening in LA."

Hunter said, "He wouldn't try to impersonate a Border Patrol Agent, it'd be too risky."

I said, "Yeah, the uniform would clash with his hair."

Hunter and Mickey frowned at me. The corners of Hondo's mouth went up a quarter inch.

"Okay," I held my hands up, "No more hair jokes."

"Why would it be too risky?" Mickey asked.

"A couple reasons, the big one being it's a felony to impersonate a federal officer. I'm surprised New Mexico didn't file on him for impersonating a police officer."

Mickey said, "He had that worked out. See, Bob was friends with the Governor and got himself appointed as special officer of the state, working undercover. Made it all legal. He also did a recruitment commercial for the State Troopers for free, his way of paying back the Governor."

Hunter said, "I doubt he could do the same for a federal job. My guess is he was going to check out some smuggling organizations on his own, like freelance."

Mickey said, "He's got a Private Investigator's license, so I guess that would make it legal, wouldn't it?"

I said, "He's got a license?"

"Uh-huh. The President of the California Association of Private Investigators gave him an honorary license."

I looked at Hondo, "This guy's got more honorary awards than Bill Cosby."

Mickey sniffed, "And he deserves every one of them. He does a lot of things for people."

"I didn't mean anything by it, Mickey. Just thinking out loud."

Hondo said, "Any of you think about the coincidences we're talking about here?" He ticked them off on his fingers, "We've got the photo of Bob at the ridge overlooking the canyon where the Mexican women were hiding; the women were smuggled there, Bob's preparing for a Border Patrol part, and we know Bob tries to authenticate what his character's going to do by doing it himself."

Hunter continued it, "So he tries to find the smuggler or smugglers of the women."

Mickey said, "And he disappears."

I said, "Let's get that photo worked on. I want to know who's there with him."

**

Hondo had a friend who ran his own security company and had lots of high tech equipment to process videos and images. I had Hondo take my windbreaker and drop it at the cleaners as he took the photo to the friend's office. It took the guy an hour to enlarge and enhance the corner of the photo that contained the shadow and the leg and foot.

Hondo brought it back to the office and when Mickey saw it she squealed, "That's a cowboy boot."

It was. A black, pointy-toed cowboy boot with a silver cap on the toe, but I didn't think it was anything to get all quivery about. I said, "Uh-huh. And the shadow is of someone standing out of camera range."

Mickey clutched at my arm, "No-no-no, you don't understand. I know that boot."

She was scared. I said, "Who is it?"

"It's Mr. Meadows' personal assistant, that Mr. Rakes."

"Carl Rakes?"

"That's him," she shivered. "He was always staring at me. He reminds me of one of those creepy guys you see in those old black and white monster movies."

Hondo said, "Were he and Bob friends?"

"No, but Bob would talk to Mr. Rakes when they were in the same room, sort of polite conversation."

I indicated the picture, "Why would Bob be there with Rakes?"

Mickey said, "I don't know. It doesn't seem to fit."

Hunter said, "Figure out who that shadow belongs to and you might have an answer."

Hunter's cell phone rang and she answered it, then moved into the storeroom to talk. When she came out she said, "I need to run. There's something extra they want me for at the LA office. Seems they want the conversation with the woman in Durango on tape."

"Smuggling?" Hondo said.

"Sounds like it. Supposed to be something they've been trying to get a handle on for a while. They think this might be part of it." She rose and said, "Later," and went out the door.

We sat a few minutes mulling things over, then Hondo said, "I think we need to pay old Carl a visit, quiz him a little about this photo."

Mickey clapped her hands together like an excited five year old, "Yes, I'm ready!"

I said, "Mickey, we'd better go this one alone." Her smile fell and tears started forming. "No, no," I said, "It's just that we expect to find him in a strip club and we don't want to expose you to that stuff. You can be more help away from places like that."

She came over and hugged my neck, then went to Hondo and did the same. "You two are my heroes, for real. I'll go now so you can do what you need to. Thank you, thank you so much." She began to cry as she left and closed the door.

"Well," Hondo said. "You always have a way with women, I'll say that for you."

"Mickey's a man."

"Not in her heart."

I looked at the door. "You're right," I said.

**

I took the three Berettas from the storeroom and disabled the firing pins. We'd decided to give them back as a gesture, but I didn't want to turn a meeting into the OK Corral if I could help it.

Besides, *our* firing pins were working and I liked that edge. We grabbed some cokes since we hadn't had a chance to eat and sipped on them while Hondo drove us in his Mercedes to The Caspian Diamond, figuring to start where I'd last seen Rakes. I started to take a sip and got a call on my cell phone. It was the repair shop and my truck was ready.

The body man said, "Never used so much Bond-O in my life. I coulda repaired the friggin' Titanic there was so much."

I said, "Are you going to charge me for the smart comments too, or just the repair work?"

"Hardy har-har, Baca. Pick it up when you're ready. I'll send you the bill so you don't have a heart attack in my office."

I told him I'd be by later to get it.

We were almost to the Diamond when Hondo said, "Talked to Archie this morning after I worked out. He said you drive Shamu to compensate for a small penis."

I spit coke, "He said what? What does he think that Corvette of his stands for?"

"Arch said it's an offshoot of his virility. He said it's not a substitute but a natural occurrence, like a smile shows teeth. I think he's right about that."

"Oh you do, huh. Well, what about this Mercedes, what's Arch say about that?"

"He said it doesn't mean anything because I won it."

"Oh, that's just great."

"Hey, it's just an observation. Doesn't have to be what you think."

I took a swig of coke and said, "Arch better watch his protein drinks or they're going to have a full charge of ex-lax giving him an unexpected thrill. Small penis my butt."

We pulled into the lot of the Caspian Diamond and parked with the other two dozen or so cars. Carl was sitting by himself at the bar and we took the stools on either side of him.

I said, "Hey Carl, you ever notice the word *glasnost* sounds like somebody having a snot-sneeze?"

He looked in the mirror at us. If it had been only one, I think the fight would have been on. Carl said, "Baca, you fuckshid, you vant something? I crack your face and ead your skull hairs if you shove me."

"He's got a way with words," I said to Hondo. I took out the Berettas and laid them on the bar in front of Rakes. "Some of your buddies dropped these and we thought we'd bring them back."

You could see the wheels spinning. But he wasn't stupid and he relaxed, putting his forearms on the bar. Carl said, "Speak what you say to hear from me."

Hondo placed the photo on the bar and said, "Tell us about this."

"Is picture of Landman."

"Yeah, and you're standing with him and there are two other people with you: One that makes the shadow and the one taking the photo. We'd like to know who they are."

"Why I tell you?"

"So we will leave you alone."

He sneered, "You don't scare Carl."

I said, "Fleas don't scare you either, but if you get them on you, they'll irritate and pester you from now on. Just think of us as a couple of pesky fleas you can get rid of with a little talk."

Carl thought about it, then said, "Was Bond and Valdar. Bond is shadow, Valdar was camera."

Hondo said, "Why'd you throw Landman's bike off the cliff?"

Carl looked in the mirror and his eyes held on Hondo. "I do not throw, what you say...bike."

"Sure you did. Wasn't anybody else there strong enough to flip it that far. C'mon, you can tell us."

The mirror showed dark shapes assembling behind us. Simon Mortay, cane in his hands, appeared behind Hondo and said, "Is enough, gentlemen. You leave now. Baca, I told you never to come back, and here are you so soon after I tell you." He shook his head, "I vill run out from pat-i-ence if you come again." The shadows materialized into the three men from our bathroom dance. They took the pistols off the bar. They held the pistols in their hands instead of holstering them.

Hondo turned to face Simon and stepped from the bar. Simon's hands blurred and there was a flicker of reflected light as he placed the needle point of a slim sword against Hondo's chest. Simon's other hand held the rest of the cane that had sheathed the blade. The hair on my neck stood up. Mortay was *fast*.

Hondo said, "Get that off my chest."

"My, we have *two* machako men here."

Hondo said, "It's macho. Learn the word before you try to use it."

My heart thumped fast and I was angry, too. What was with these people? I said, "Simon, we asked Carl a few questions and we're ready to leave. You can put your shiskebob maker back in its holder."

"Or what?"

I looked at him, "You ever watch Sam Peckinpah movies? It'll be like that."

Simon started to speak and Hondo interrupted him, "I told you once, get that off me."

Something in Hondo's voice got Simon's attention. Carl then said something in Russian and Simon glanced at the three pistol-toters. He barked an order and one of them, the red-eyed one, pointed his Beretta at the bar and pulled the trigger. It clicked.

That changed the atmosphere. Simon nodded, sheathed his sword cane and held it across his thighs. "You should go."

Hondo had his Glock in his hand. I hadn't seen him draw.

"Ask us to stay and we'll leave," he said.

I moved to Hondo's side and whispered, "What are you doing? Let's get out of here."

"If he asks us to stay, then we'll leave."

"Look, there's a lot of them, maybe more in the back."

"I'm not going until he asks."

"Are you willing to get us killed just because you were insulted?" Hondo looked at me and then back at Simon. I'd read the answer.

I said, "Simon, ask us to stay and we'll leave."

"I tell you to *go*. Now."

Hondo raised the Glock and pointed it between Simon's eyes. People beside him stepped away. The black hole on the .45 must have looked like a cave to Simon, and I watched him swallow. My heart banged against my ribs. I said, "Simon, just ask us to stay."

Carl said something to Simon in Russian and Simon's lips thinned, then he said, "Perhaps you would like to stay."

Hondo lowered his Glock but didn't holster it and said, "No thanks, we've got to be going."

**

As we drove away Hondo said, "You want something to eat?"

"Maybe you could take me by the ER, get them to jumpstart my heart."

"It's over now, just relax and enjoy the day."

"He's not going to forget that."

Hondo said, "I bet not."

We stopped and ate Chinese and took an extra helping of Kung Pao Chicken with us for Hunter. Hondo dropped me off at the repair shop and I told him I'd be right along.

I got the keys for Shamu and looked the pickup over before I got in. They had done a good job. Not a single bullet hole showed. I started her up and hit the road. Five minutes later, I saw a Volkswagen painted up with southwestern scenes zip by in the opposite direction. Mickey was in a hurry and didn't see me as I waved. I parked in the gym's lot and heard Archie yell at me from the door, "I thought I smelled fish." He was wearing a sweatshirt with the sleeves cut out and his arms looked as brown and hard as carved oak.

I said, "You'll think fish, you keep insulting my wheels." He cackled and waved and closed the door.

Hunter wasn't back so Hondo called her cell phone and left a message that we were going home and we'd see her in the morning. We left and as I drove Shamu, I felt the fatigue really hit me. Dealing with swords and guns will tire you out, I guarantee.

CHAPTER EIGHT

I was up before sunrise and jogging my five-mile loop as the eastern sky backlit the mountains in shades of orange. I thought about who Carl Rakes said were the others in the picture: Bond and Valdar. I wasn't ready to talk to Bond, and Valdar wasn't anywhere I could reach him without a good psychic, so where to go with the info I had? After another half mile, the name Deco Martinez popped into my head. The gang member turned artist, friend of Valdar and Bob Landman. Deco Martinez had also been written on the note we found in Landman's' fanny pack, but in the jumble of words, I had assumed they were two different items, not a name. Now, as I pictured the note I could see that Landman had written Deco Martinez as a name, then the other words were half on top of it, which resulted in the confusion.

It was a good place to start the day. I kicked up the pace and started back to the house. After a shower and slice of toast and orange juice, I was in Shamu and driving down Mulholland. I called the office and Hondo didn't answer so I left a message that I was going to check out Deco. I drove into Beverly Hills and stopped again at Pelson's Galleries to talk to Harold about how best to contact Martinez. Harold was finishing with a customer when I arrived and I studied several of the paintings while I waited. When Harold finished he came over.

I pointed at a colorful canvas about the size of a sheet of typing paper and asked, "How much is this one?"

"Two-ten."

"Two hundred and ten dollars? That sounds cheap."

"It is cheap, but it's two hundred and ten thousand dollars."

I grabbed my chest in a mock heart attack. "I guess I'll keep the decor of my home in Early Plastic."

Harold smiled and said, "What can I do for you, Investigator Ronny?"

"I need to talk with Deco Martinez. Any suggestions?"

"I have his studio address and can call as an introduction. I don't think you'd be able to see him otherwise, maybe not even then. Deco is a strange fellow. When did you want to visit him?"

"Today."

"Come back to my office and I'll call." I followed him and he reached Deco's assistant on the first try. He tried every persuasion, but was told that Deco wouldn't see anyone. Harold walked me to the door and said, "I'm sorry. Artists are a strange breed, and the ones here in Los Angeles are the strangest of the strange."

"No problem. Thanks for trying."

"What will you do now?"

"Hey, I'm a trained professional, practically unstoppable when I get after something. I'll go to Plan B."

"Plan B means you don't have a clue, is that right?"

I arched an eyebrow at him, "Ah-ha, so you're a trained professional, too."

**

I sat in Shamu for a while and thought I might try a long shot. I drove from Beverly Hills through downtown Los Angeles and into East LA, heading for the Hotel Camino Real and hoping to find some of my newest acquaintances. Who knows, I might find Elvis too, down for a little visit with Loomis.

I saw them in a vacant lot two blocks west of the hotel. Pretty Boy and Chato were leaning against the fender of a nice looking 77 Ford Fairlane, the big beer bottles hanging from their fingers. I parked Shamu thirty feet away and walked to them.

Pretty Boy looked at my truck, "They fixed the holes in your whale, uh? Looks good, ese."

I said, "You guys know who Deco Martinez is?"

"Si-mon," He pronounced it see-*moan*, "Deco's a Home-Boy who made it good. He's a famous painter, Holmes."

"I know. Is he Maravilla?"

"Damn straight. He used to date my tia."

"You think you could arrange it so I could talk to him?"

Pretty Boy cocked his head to the side, "What for, Holmes?"

"I think he might have some information I need."

He took a pull off the bottle and said, "I'll talk to him. When you want to do it?"

"The sooner the better."

"Tell me when and where and I'll have him come by this afternoon."

"You don't need to check with him first?"

He shook his head at me like I didn't understand, "The Maravilla are tight, Holmes. I tell him you saved our lives and he'll be there."

"Okay," I gave him the office address and said, "Three would be good."

"*Hecho*, it's done."

I thanked them and walked to my truck. Chato said something to Pretty Boy that got him laughing. I said, "What?"

"Holmes, Chato said we should paint a big fish-hook coming out of the mouth of your whalemobile."

Even gangbangers are comedians these days.

**

I had the office to myself that afternoon. Hunter was with the ICE office in the Federal Building on North Los Angeles Street and Hondo was digging through more files to find who owned the Russian clubs. Deco Martinez came in right at three. He was a scowling, big shouldered man over six feet tall, with long dark hair that had a reddish tinge.

He said, "You Baca?"

"The one and only."

"Private Investigator, huh?" I nodded. He said, "What is it you want to know?" I pointed to a chair and he sat.

I said, "I'm trying to find Bob Landman, the actor, and I'm having no luck doing it."

His right eye made the tiniest tic when I said Landman's name. He said, "So?"

"I know you were at some recent parties with him and Valdar, so I thought maybe you'd seen or heard from him in the last few days."

"Valdar's dead."

"Well, they haven't found a body yet."

"There was too much blood. Trust me, he's dead."

He was there. I sat a little straighter, "You want to expand on that?"

He got up, shaking his head, "This shit is way beyond you, Baca. You don't want any part of it."

"Why'd you beat him, you and your buddies?"

"We didn't do anything to him." He rubbed his chin, then said, "We got there too late."

"So, you were going there to beat him up but somebody beat you to it, pardon the pun."

"You are *so* over your head here."

I was hearing *You don't know shit* again in a little different phrasing. I said, "Why don't you fill me in? I've been hearing that all week."

Deco looked at me, and for a moment I thought he might spill it all. Instead, he sighed, "I'm not out to hurt Landman, know that first. But there are people involved that..."

"That what?"

He rubbed his chin, then said, "They're bad people."

"Come on, Deco. You're a Maravilla, one of the toughest gangs in Los Angeles. What do you mean, 'They're bad people'? Bad compared to who, the Maravilla? Give me a break."

"The Maravilla are a family, Baca. We do what we do to hold our barrio together, to protect each other and to keep our honor. We're nothing like these others."

"Like how?"

"They are merciless, without morals or scruples, and they only desire money and power."

"So they're Democrats and Republicans."

Deco looked like he tasted something sour. "You won't be joking if you keep messing in this. Landman crossed their path, started sniffing around, and now no one can find him."

"Is he alive?"

"Lots of people still hunting for him. They don't hunt for dead people."

"Who is 'They'?"

Deco looked at me, "How do you make a living?"

"The mark of a true professional is to look like they're not doing anything."

"Well, you've got that down." He glanced out the window, then turned back and said, "Organized crime. That's who 'They' is."

"All organized crime?"

Deco sighed, "In LA. Mexican Mafia, Russians, those guys."

"What did Landman do to stir them up?"

"He was nosing around and found something."

I took a long shot, "Did it have to do with something in the shoebox you took?"

The skin around Deco's eyes grew white and for a moment, I thought he might have a stroke. "You can't know that!"

I crossed my arms on my chest and said, "I'm the Karnak of Investigators. I see all, I hear all."

He was agitated now, "This is no game, Baca. That information could get us both killed."

"What was in the box?"

"I can't tell you." Even as Martinez said it, I could see him considering the idea. This guy carried a load on his shoulders and was feeling all alone.

I took one of my cards and wrote my home phone and cell phone numbers on it. I had to hold it out to him until my shoulder burned before he finally took it. "You call me when you want to talk. Ask Pretty Boy, I can be trusted."

He left with the card, but not before looking out the window at the parking lot for a good minute. I put my feet up on the desk and chewed on a pencil. This was starting to get like a fifties spy movie, all Thems and Theys and vague threats and furtive characters. Not me though, I wasn't a furtive character. I was the guy who figured out everything. I just didn't know when that part would start.

**

Hondo showed up at five PM with some limes, a saltshaker, and a six pack of Tecate in the cans. He opened two cans and took out his SOG knife to cut a lime into quarter wedges. I started to speak but he said, "Get one down, then we'll talk."

We squeezed the lime wedges into and onto the can openings, then sprinkled it with salt. I hadn't drunk Tecate in a while and it was cold and crisp, with the mixtures of salt and lime juice combining with each swallow.

We finished our cans and Hondo made us two more before he talked.

Hondo said, "Ever hear of Sakhalin?"

"Yeah, it's an island off the coast of Russia. I think it's a military base, something like that."

"Uh-huh. The one that shot down a loaded Japanese passenger jet that got over their air space."

"That happened a good while back."

"Yeah, before the USSR collapsed."

"And?"

"Simon Mortay was the one who gave the order to shoot it down."

"He was a Soviet officer?"

"Yep. A rising star until that fiasco. Afterward he was shuffled to different assignments, then disappeared for a few years."

"And now he's here, working for the Russian Mafia."

"Bingo."

"Hey," I said, "I thought you were researching property titles. How'd you wind up with this stuff?"

"Oh, on a hunch I called a friend."

"What kind of friend knows stuff like that?"

"You know."

I nodded, "Uh-huh. A friend from your third world days."

"I was working as a candle maker then."

"Uh-huh," I said. "Gave a bunch of those folks in that area a whole new meaning to 'light me up'."

Hondo spread his hands. "Mortay's not the big honcho, but he's important. It's assumed Mortay's using old military contacts to do some smuggling into the United States."

"Smuggling what?"

"They'll get back to me on that. Could be anything."

"I hear Boris Yeltsin Life-size Love Dolls are big this year."

Hondo drank the last of his second beer and said, "Yep, right along with the children's working model Chernobyl Reactor, complete with real radioactive core. I hear it's good for ages ten and up."

"That's a Gotta-Have if I ever heard one. What's the box look like?"

"It's color, shows two kids with no teeth and hair falling out playing with the glowing reactor. Thing's a real eye-catcher."

"Too bad we don't have kids, huh?"

"Too bad."

Hunter walked in at that moment and saw us both with cans in our hands. She went to the small refrigerator and got herself one while Hondo cut another lime. She doctored the opening with salt and lime juice and took a long swallow as she sat on the edge of Hondo's desk. She said, "Oh, that is fine." She looked at us, "That all you two did today, sit around and drink beer while I worked my buns off?"

I angled my head to look at her rear, "You didn't work them *all* off. There's a goodly portion left."

"Goodly," Hondo said.

Hunter looked under her arm at her rear, "Yeah, I'm getting flabby."

I almost choked on my beer. Hunter's rear is about as flabby as the butt on an Olympic gymnast. You could bounce quarters off it.

"You come up with anything?" Hondo asked.

Hunter said, "Some. I read through the ICE reports before the woman called, then quizzed her about some of the points. Seems there's a regular pipeline smuggling young, pretty women from Mexico into California, especially the LA area. The woman said a man recruited her daughter and several relatives, and he went from village to village to get the best looking ones and bring them up. The trick is, they don't have to pay much to be smuggled, but the smugglers gather all their wages at the jobs until they've worked off the trip."

I said, "Isn't that what we used to call indentured servitude?"

Hunter said, "Uh-huh. But knowing what I know about smugglers, if they control all the money these women earn, then the women will never finish paying off their trips."

Hondo said, "How many are they bringing in?"

"Not large numbers now, because they've expanded their operations. Maybe two dozen a month. What the smugglers have done is expand on what they're doing. The women are carrying things into the country for the smuggler, and they've been joined near the border by other people being smuggled in, and these people are Caucasians."

"What do you make of that?" I asked.

"The best guess is the Caucasians are East Europeans. They are paired with the women to pass as couples. It makes it easier to travel through the US if you're a couple."

"Were the women in the canyon part of this?"

"The woman I talked to in Mexico said she thought so."

"Why didn't we find any men?"

"Nobody knows, but my guess is the Caucasians are separated as soon as possible and sent somewhere else. They're paying a lot of money to be smuggled in, and they'll be taken care of. The women are expendable. If they get caught, they are only sent across at Tijuana, or like the ones in the canyon, documented and let go."

"What kinds of things are the women carrying into the country? Is it narcotics?"

"No, it sounds like jewels and gold artifacts."

Hondo and I looked at each other. I said, "So, they must be stolen or the smugglers could bring them through Customs." Hunter said, "Uh-huh. What they found, two Border Patrol Agents near El Campo worked a canyon north of town and found a woman who had been stabbed and left for dead. Her last statements were of carrying a wrapped package and that she was killed because she peeked inside."

Hondo asked, "Did she say what was inside?"

Hunter took a sip of Tecate and looked at Hondo for several seconds, then at me, "The woman said it was a golden egg, covered with green, red and white jewels."

Hondo and I were silent as it sunk in. "A Faberge egg?" I said.

"What it sounds like," Hunter said. "That was the last thing she said before dying."

"Ho-ly shit," I said.

"Even if it's a copy, they had to be smuggling it in because it was stolen," Hondo said.

"And each woman was carrying something?" I said.

Hunter nodded. "So, about two dozen pieces a month over the last year."

I said, "Be nice to know if that egg was original. We could narrow things down pretty fast then."

Hunter said, "Yep. That's the only account we have, and it doesn't describe in detail what the egg looked like."

Hondo said, "Well, with what I found out today about the Russians involved in smuggling, and Faberge eggs are Russian, maybe we can start there, see where it takes us."

Hunter said, "Sure, but after we eat. I'm starving."

**

We went to a place in Santa Monica on Entrada Drive that served good chicken fajitas and nachos and we continued our talks, but switched to iced tea to drink. I paid for the meals and we went back to the office, getting there about seven PM.

The answering machine light was blinking on the phone and Hondo pushed the PLAY button. Mickey's excited, breathless voice came over the speaker, "Ronny, Hondo, I've been checking into some things and I think I'm *really* on to something! I'll be sleuthing this evening and I'll fill you in tomorrow morning. If it works out to what I think, you'll be *so* excited! It will help us find Bob, and answer a lot of questions, too. I know, I know, I'll be careful. Talk to you tomorrow. Bye-bye."

I picked up the phone and called Mickey's cell phone, but got no answer. I left a message for her to call, then called every other number for her and got no answers on any of them. I left messages on them all and hung up after the last one. I said, "Mickey's going to get a real chewing out when we see her again."

Hondo said, "She was too excited not to have found something."

"Yep."

We sat in silence for a moment, then Hunter said, "Not much sleep tonight, huh?"

**

It was ten o'clock the next morning before we heard something, and it wasn't Mickey. Sergeant Vick Best called and I answered.

Best said, "Ronny, we found one of your business cards this morning."

A sinking feeling settled in my stomach. Hondo and Hunter watched me. I said, "Where?"

"You know somebody named Mickey Haile?"

I closed my eyes and nodded. Hondo whispered, "Oh, man."

I said, "Yeah, where is she?"

"She? It's a man, Ronny, wearing a woman's clothes."

I said, "Where is Mickey?"

After a second Vick said, "It's a body. A bicyclist found it this morning. We're on Mulholland Highway, a mile west of where it intersects with Old Topanga Canyon Road."

"We're headed that way."

"Ronny, it's not pretty. If you'd rather talk-"

"We're on our way." I hung up as Hondo pulled the keys from his pocket.

**

There were a dozen law enforcement vehicles parked along the shoulder of the road and twenty yards from the pavement, we saw the yellow crime scene tape outlining a draw that angled up into the mountains.

Vick saw us coming and lifted up the tape. He said, "They've finished gathering forensics and we'll be taking the body in a few minutes."

He led us into the draw and I saw Mickey. She was wearing her pink and green biking clothes and was lying on her stomach on the talus in the bottom. Her face was toward us and was almost unrecognizable. Someone had beaten her until all the bones were broken. I walked to the body and knelt down. The fingers on her right hand had been broken and there were a dozen holes the size of grapes over the backs of her legs. The holes weren't round, but oval, like someone inserted a slim blade and moved it around the way you use a stick to stir paint. She'd been alive when they finished. Dried blood left tracks like red roads from each wound along her legs, indicating she had moved, or been moved, while she bled.

Hondo squatted beside me and looked for several seconds. He pointed at the holes in her legs. "These are at nerve clusters. Pain would have been the kind to pop your skull off."

I said, "They aren't bullet holes."

"Nope."

We looked at Mickey for several more minutes, then climbed out to join Vick. He called over the primary Investigator and had him stand with us and ask his questions. We answered them and when we mentioned the phone message from last night, Vick looked at the ground and shook his head.

"Haile shouldn't have tried to do it alone."

"I know."

Hondo said, "Crime Scene people come up with anything?"

"Doesn't look like it. We couldn't even find any tracks down to the body."

Hunter stepped closer and pointed at the ground beside us, "Looks like a couple people here went straight to the edge and came back. You can see where they walked over their own tracks." I looked where she was pointing and couldn't see anything. There was little soil, only the faintest dusting over the gravel and exposed rock. I lifted my foot and looked where it had been and couldn't see that I'd ever stood there.

Vick said, "Border Patrol, a tracker, right?"

Hunter nodded. "You want me to take a look?"

"Yeah."

Hunter said, "I'll need to take a look at the soles of whoever walked around here."

Vick motioned over the investigator and several others. The Crime Scene people had left but Vick said they were wearing Reeboks, if that helped. Hunter checked everyone's shoes, including ours, then walked to the body.

We moved to the side and watched her. Hunter took her time, studying a three-sixty around the body and working in ever-larger concentric circles out of the draw. It took fifteen minutes before she reached the pavement. Hunter turned to look at the body and rubbed the back of her neck. She studied the terrain for a moment, then went to the edge of the draw and knelt. She nodded to herself, rose, and walked to us.

"Nobody took Mickey into the draw. They…no, make that he--threw her into it from the edge."

I looked from the edge to the body. The killer threw her away like trash.

Vick said, "You sure?"

Hunter nodded. "Two people went from the road to the edge of the draw and the long striding one was carrying the body." Hunter pointed at a spot. "He threw Mickey from there, got his legs into it and scrooched the gravel with his foot as he pushed off, kind of like somebody throwing the shot put. It left a small pressure ridge in the ground where his left foot rotated in the follow through, so my guess is he's right handed. They probably weren't out of the car more than thirty seconds before they were rolling again."

The investigator was writing as Hunter talked. He said, "I may have to call you as a witness on this."

Hunter said, "No problem. I've done it before."

Vick asked if there was anything else we wanted to add, and we shook our heads. He waved the men down with the body bag and they put Mickey's tiny broken form inside and zipped it up.

Hunter said in a hoarse voice, "I think I'll go back to the car." I noticed Hondo had put on his sunglasses.

I bit the inside of my cheek to get control and said to Vick, "We think of anything, we'll get in touch."

Vick looked at me, "You remember that. We'll be on this and do what needs to be done. Don't interfere in the investigation, Ronny. That goes for you too, Hondo. I mean it."

I said, "We're working on finding Bob Landman."

Vick said, "Yeah, but you and I both know this is all tied together, and *we're* looking for Landman. Don't get in the way."

I turned and walked to the Mercedes with Hondo. Before we drove away, Hondo put up the top on the convertible. He said, "Too much blue sky and sunshine right now. It should be raining."

Hunter tapped my shoulder and said, "Can I borrow your handkerchief?" She'd put on Ray Bans like Hondo and her nose was red. I gave her my handkerchief and wished I had brought my own sunglasses. With the top up, I couldn't even say the wind was causing my eyes to water.

CHAPTER NINE

As we drove away, I said to Hondo, "You remember Mickey's home address?"

He looked at me and nodded.

Hunter said, "Yeah, maybe there's something we can find."

"You can't go." I said.

"I sure can. You watch me."

Hondo said, "No, Hunter. If Vick or his people walk in on us, it'll be your career. We can't let you risk it."

"But-"

"No Buts," I said. "We'll drop you at the office and fill you in when we get back."

"Or call you for bail money," Hondo said.

I said, "Besides, Hondo and I can go through the place almost as fast as the three of us could. You know that. Three's almost too many for a small house."

She didn't say yes, but she didn't disagree anymore. We were silent as Hondo drove us to the office, where Hunter got out and Hondo turned toward West Hollywood.

**

Mickey's house was small white stucco on the corner, with a large eucalyptus tree in the front yard whose roots were cracking the sidewalk. We parked in the drive and walked to the door. I tried the knob.

"It's locked."

Hondo moved me out of the way and fiddled with it for several seconds and the door opened. He said, "Nah, just stuck a little from the humidity." I didn't remind him we were in the middle of a drought.

The inside was neat, with peach colored walls and a white leather sofa and armchair. The floor was tile and the kitchen had a six-foot bar with barstools around it for the eating area. A tall, wide computer desk and filing cabinets took up the place for the dining room table. Hondo turned on the computer and we watched the screen come up with a floating message of hot pink script letters: *Give yourself a Great Day!*

Hondo punched some keys and the Windows screen came up. I said, "Go ahead. I'll look around the rest of the house." Hondo nodded and I walked down a hall and into the single bedroom. There was a canopy bed made in soft pinks and whites, with furry teddy bears lying on the made-up bed. I went to the nightstand beside the bed and opened the drawer below the phone. Inside was a diary with a lock.

I took it out and found the tiny key underneath the book. I opened the lock and flipped through the pages until I got to the last entries and started with three days ago.

Dear Diary, I got a call today from the Sheriff's Department to go to Bobby's Malibu home and pick up some things they wanted out of there. I thought about calling Ronny and Hondo, but felt I could do it on my own and show them I'm good for something. I admire them so much. They are the finest, most noble men I have ever known. Bob is a great person and I love him with all my heart (Yes Dear Diary, even if we haven't kissed!), but Ronny and Hondo are so...well, Heroic. But they aren't stiff or anything, just funny and warm and kind. If anybody can find Bobby, they will. Oh, I hope so!

The next entry read:

Dear Diary, What a great discovery! I can't believe it was in front of us all this time. It will be so easy now to get Bobby! I'll have to be careful, though. I saw The Ghoul driving by my house again today, and this time he stopped in front and sat in his car for over an hour. He scares me sooo much! I've decided not to tell Ronny about this and am going to find my Bobby without them. I need to show them I'm not helpless, not a twitter head. I need to see myself as more in their eyes. For me.

The last entry was scribbled in a hurry:

Dear Diary, I'm going today. The Ghoul followed me yesterday when I left, and I wonder if he didn't follow me when the Sheriff's Department let me pick up things from Bobby's Malibu home. He is totally frightening.

Going now. Called Ronny's office and left the message. (Dear Diary, they will be sooo impressed!) I'll go out the back and over the fence so The Ghoul doesn't see me (Yes DD, he's sitting across the street). I'm so scared I'm shaking all over, but am going through with this anyhow.

PS: I wish I was like Hunter Kincaid, so beautiful and not afraid of anything---I can't wait to see my Bobby!

I put the diary down and stood in silence for a minute.

Hondo called from the other room, "Sheriff's department just pulled up out front."

I wiped down the drawer and the diary and key and put it back, then went into the walk-in closet to see if what Mickey had brought from Malibu was there and saw dozens of framed photos leaning against the wall. They were of Bob Landman with other actors and several politicians. Further down were a dozen or so of Valdar's paintings stacked against each other. I started toward them when Hondo said behind me, "Time to go."

I followed him to the kitchen and we went out the back door only seconds before we heard the front door open. Hondo led us across the tiny back yard and into the alley, where we went up several blocks and found a convenience store.

We thumbed through magazines, drank coffee, and read the newspapers from cover to cover as we waited for the investigators to finish with Mickey's house, not to go back inside but to get to our car, which so far had escaped their notice. The store manager was eyeing us as I paid for two cokes and two bags of peanut M&Ms. We'd been in his store for an hour and he wasn't sure if we were homeless or were going to rob him.

Hondo walked up the street and glanced toward Mickey's house. As I watched through the storefront window, Hondo gave me the Come-On hand wave.

I picked up a pack of Doublemint gum and took it to the manager at the counter. "You passed," I said.

He frowned and his mouth opened a little.

I pulled out my identification and flipped it in front of his face too fast for him to get anything more than a glimpse. "Company investigators, Quality Control. You did a bang-up job working the register and dusting. Good finger skills," I winked at him, "We'll be dropping your name in for Manager of the Month."

A big smile broke out on his face. When I tried to pay for the gum, he waved a hand at me and said, "On the house."

I took the gum and went outside. Hondo was already at his car and I walked halfway down the street before he drove up and I got in. I gave him a stick of gum.

"I have to peel it, too?"

I took it back from him, peeled the paper, and gave it back. "You find anything on the computer?"

"I took her thumb drive and downloaded some of the last things she had run, but I didn't have time to get everything. I figure it'll be safer to check when we're at the office. You find anything in the bedroom?"

I told him about the diary and he nodded as he put on his sunglasses. He said, "In front of us all the time. What is it, you got any idea?"

"I didn't have time to look at everything she brought from Malibu, but her diary didn't mention discovery until she got the stuff, so I figure it was in that batch of goodies."

"Was it paintings and photos?"

"How'd you know that?"

"I saw the investigator taking that stuff out of Mickey's house and putting it in his car."

I thought, then nodded, "Mickey was to hold the items and now Mickey's gone, so the Sheriff's Department will have to take it back in custody."

"Uh-huh."

"We can't go to Vick and ask to go through them."

"Yep."

"We'll need to get pictures or copies or something."

"Uh-huh."

I turned to him, "Any ideas how we can do that?"

Hondo reached into his shirt pocket and took out the floppy. "I think Mickey took photos of everything for an inventory and we've got it right here, or at least most of it."

"World class investigator, that's you."

"It's amazing what you can find doing a little B&E."

**

At the office, Hondo found our computer's photo software wasn't compatible with that on Mickey's disk, so he went out to buy something that would work. Hunter had left a message that she was with Immigration and would be back later. I was alone, and I propped my feet up and thought about The Ghoul. Hondo and I had talked about who it might be, but we didn't know everyone Mickey knew, so it was difficult. I could only think of one person to ask. Bond Meadows.

I decided to check the house in Beverly Hills first, then go from there if it didn't pan out. I didn't call because I didn't want her to tell me I couldn't come in. I've found surprise visits work well with people who don't want to see you.

I punched in the number at the mansion's gate and was glad Bond hadn't changed it since she'd fired me. I drove into the drive, parked by the door, and rang the bell.

There was no answer so I tried the knob and found it open. I walked in and said, "Hello," but got no reply. I listened for any sounds but heard nothing, so I walked the long floor to the backyard and stopped at the French doors to look through the glass at the pool area.

Carl Rakes was wearing a black Speedo and catching rays in a lounge chair, with Bond next to him feeding him grapes by holding them in her lips and pressing her mouth to his. Iced champagne cooled under the umbrella, and glasses rested near their hands. A third glass was by an adjacent chair and I didn't have long to figure out who else was there because old iron grip himself, Frank Meadows walked out carrying what looked like a silver tray of chocolate covered strawberries that he sat near Bond, then put his chair on the other side of Rakes.

Now wasn't this a fine situation? I watched some more as Bond fed Carl grapes and strawberries and ran her hands over his tats. They were talking but I was too far to make out what they were saying and I'd never been good at lip reading, unless you count the swearing done by NFL coaches on the sidelines. Beyond the pool area were the topiary shapes of the animals. Behind them, the small jungle of manicured bushes and trees extended to the ten-foot high rock wall surrounding the property. I noticed the wall had a security system along the top to catch anyone climbing over, but I also remembered the security control box was by the front door, so I turned and retraced my route through the house.

The security system control panel opened with a pull, for which I was grateful. Every switch was labeled. I thought it was funny that the only one switched on was the one around the back yard. All the others were turned off. No wonder I could drive up and waltz right through the door. I flipped the last switch to Off and went out the door.

I drove out and parked down the street behind several landscaping trucks. Using the trucks for cover, I trotted to the Meadows' privacy wall and pulled myself over, dropping against the inside, where the bushes hid me. I stayed low through the bushes and it was easy going. Everything was mulched to perfection and I was as silent as a ghost as I approached the pool area.

Their voices became audible, then cleared as I reached the last edge of topiary by the cement area surrounding the pool.

I was behind the twelve-foot high mother kangaroo and joey in her pouch, but couldn't quite make out all the words they said, so I wormed my way into the foliage.

My head popped out beside the joey.

I was glad no one from funniest home videos was filming. The joey's leafy head partially shielded me and I could peer through in places where the branches were dead and brittle.

Bond was eating a strawberry while Carl held a glass of champagne for her to sip as she nibbled on the chocolate tip. Frank was tanking down his champagne in gulps. He paid them no attention and scratched his bare brown stomach.

Frank burped and said, "So you think that'll stop it."

Carl handed the glass to Bond and turned to Frank, "Dah, was finish."

Bond said, "Frank, don't piss your pants over this. Now's not the time to get squeamish." As Bond talked, she ran her fingernails across the front of Carl's Speedo.

Frank didn't even blink, "What I'm saying, suppose those assholes don't quit, suppose the police find something? Then what?"

Carl rumbled, "Is not to vorry. I take care of this, for my pleasure."

Frank said, "But-"

"No 'But', I take care. You do for what I say. Things vill be good."

Bond rose from her chair went to Frank, bent over and kissed him. I pushed the joey's ear out of the way and got a view of Bond's thong. She might have been a bitch, but all those hours on the Stairmaster and doing pelvic thrusts had paid off. I had to strain to hear her words as she talked to Frank.

"Frank, baby, Carl hasn't let us down yet, right?" Frank nodded and Bond continued, "Things will get better now that we've gotten past this little bump in the road. Besides, the police have to play by rules. We don't."

Carl said, "Dah, now to find shidmouth hair actor, then we go back to the business."

Frank said, "What about Baca and Wells, and that other one, the Border Patrol woman?"

Bond snorted, "Frank, I fired them, remember? The woman's only here for a few days and she'll be gone. We'll find Bob. Besides, Baca's not that good."

Not that good? What way did she mean that?

"He's the kind that doesn't work if he's not getting paid. If he'd actually found Bob, we'd be through with this, but he couldn't. I thought we had him going and he would put Landman in our hands. He sure bought the Poor Me angle."

Frank said, "All I know is he pisses me off and he's always turning up unexpected. But you're right, he fell for your line of bullshit, didn't he?" Frank toasted her with his glass.

"Yeah, piece of cake." She cupped her breasts in her hands and said, "Just rubbed these on him a little bit and he only looked where I told him, till that Kincaid bitch showed up." She frowned, downed her champagne, and held the glass out to Carl to refill. Bond continued, "I know this, a dead faggot cross dresser doesn't mean anything to him, so that worry is gone." She moved and sat to face Carl and Frank and her words were muffled. I caught some words and phrases, but nothing I could put together.

I leaned forward and pushed the joey's ear further and it broke with a small, dry *crack*.

Carl sat up like a Doberman. I tried to push up the ear, but it didn't stay. Joey was now flop eared.

Carl rose and walked toward the kangaroo as I scurried backward from the bush and headed out of there. I was twenty yards from the inside corner of the ten foot high rock wall when I heard Carl reach me.

"Hah, Baca, is you!" He grasped my shoulder and I turned with his pull and hit him right on the button as hard as I've ever hit anyone.

His head went back maybe three inches.

Ohhh shit.

Carl's eyes glowed with heat. He snarled as he reached for me and I slapped his hand away and shot a punch for his throat, but he was quick and knew what he was doing and he slipped it. Behind him, I could see Frank and Bond racing for us.

I went low and kicked hard at the side of his knee and he buckled. I followed with a reverse back fist aimed for his temple but he ducked enough for it to catch his head a glancing blow.

It knocked him off balance and that was enough. I ran toward the rock wall with Carl springing up and running three strides behind me. Frank and Bond were twenty yards away and coming full tilt. I looked at a three-tiered fountain near the wall as I ran and a wild idea flashed in my head.

I cut towards it and leapt so my left foot landed on the lower tier and I pushed up so that my right foot landed on the top tier, and I jumped. The adrenaline pumped and I cleared the top of the wall without using my hands.

I hit the ground and rolled into a run while Carl screamed threats in his native tongue. As I put the wall behind me, I heard

Bond chewing Carl out in Russian. I was in Shamu and driving away in seconds.

**

Hondo and Hunter were at the office and I told them what happened, reciting the bits and pieces of conversation I heard, then asking what they thought it might mean, what words would fill in the blanks.

Hunter said, "You don't think Frank or Bond will report you to the police?"

Hondo said, "I doubt it. Ronny would have a chance to talk and might stir up the cops."

I nodded. "Too risky for them. They're into some dirty stuff, I just can't figure out what and how yet."

"They might come after you, though," Hondo said.

"They might," I said. "Meanwhile we've got a case to solve."

Hunter said, "Well I wish you'd hurry up. My vacation runs out next week and I've got to go back."

"Oh sure," I said. "The Microwave Detectives. Investigate all day in ten minutes." She threw a paper clip at me.

We sat for a moment and Hunter said, "What did you say Bond's maiden name was?"

"Savitch, why?"

She tapped her lips with her forefinger, "You heard her speak Russian, right?"

"I think that's what it was. Like what Russians sound like in those old spy movies."

Hunter rolled her eyes, then said, "I thought I might do a little research on her at the Immigration office. Could be she immigrated."

"You can do that with just a name?" I asked.

"Makes it more difficult, but there aren't many women named Bond. That'll help."

Hondo said, "And if she did?"

Hunter said, "Depends. It might show some connections from her past that will help us. While I'm at it, I'll look up Carl Rakes and see how in the hell he made it into the country. If we're lucky, he's undocumented."

I nodded. "Sounds good to me."

Hunter stood and said, "I'll probably go to Hondo's after I finish unless I find something really good."

Hondo said, "Just keep your cell phone on. They may try for you as a way to get back at Ronny."

Hunter tapped the phone on her hip, then her jacket where the shoulder holster rode. "They'll both be where I can get at them."

When Hunter was gone Hondo said, "We're going to the Caspian Diamond, I assume."

I said, "Why don't you go ahead, but watch from the parking lot until I get there. I'm going to check on something with our friend, Sergeant Best."

Hondo nodded, "See you there."

**

Vick was at the West Hollywood station on San Vicente and I knew he was happy to see me when I walked into his office.

"Baca, what the hell do you want?"

"Hey, Sergeant, good to see you, too."

"I'm busy, what?"

I leaned over his desk and looked at the yellow lined writing pad under his hand. "Are we writing something, a note to the Sheriff, perhaps, telling him how helpful those two private investigators, Baca and Wells, are? Hmmmm?"

He covered the pad with his hand. "No, smartass. If you must know, it's another speech I've got to make this afternoon with the mayor."

"Aren't we popular."

Vick sighed, "All I ever wanted to do was street work." He looked out the window and sighed again.

"I'd like to look at the paintings from Landman's Malibu house," I said.

"Why?"

"I don't know. Just a gut feeling. I won't take long, Vick. And I'm not interfering."

He squinted at me with one eye, like Popeye. "You find anything, you share, okay?"

"Deal."

We went to the evidence room and against the far wall were the paintings. Vick left a deputy with me so they wouldn't have to explain an unguarded civilian loose in the bowels of the Department. I went through them all and then started with the half-finished painting of Landman as a Border Patrol Agent standing at the bluff. I studied it for several minutes, but didn't see anything I hadn't seen before. I went through the remaining paintings and studied them one by one, hoping something would jump out at me, but nothing did. After half an hour, I stepped back and rested against a shelf. I had all the paintings lined up and facing me. I went down them one by one from left to right. Something was nagging at me, but I couldn't put my finger on it. I closed my eyes and thought through everything, then let my mind go where it wanted.

For some reason I began to see myself as a kid, sitting at the kitchen table with my parents and putting together one of those thousand-piece puzzles. I let my mind go with it, watching my younger self take two pieces out of the pile and link them together before putting them in the puzzle.

My eyes opened and I looked at the canvases. I moved one canvas beside the painting of Landman on the bluff. It was a continuation of the painting, showing a long canyon. I looked at the remaining paintings and found a third. In it, the canyon extended, and at the far end was a small cave, with several figures in the entrance. The figures all had strawberry blond hair.

**

I thanked Vick and said I wasn't sure that I had found anything, but would keep him advised. He shooed me out and returned to writing his speech.

I drove Shamu through increasing traffic toward the Caspian Diamond, eager to talk to Hondo about the paintings. It took me almost an hour to get there. A Lexus was exiting as I entered, and it squealed tires as it hit the highway. Hondo wasn't in his Mercedes. Heavy rock music seeped through the walls of the Diamond and I could hear it through my closed windows. I had a funny feeling in my stomach and parked beside Hondo's convertible. I didn't walk, I trotted toward the door. The deafening sounds of a Guns N Roses oldie, *Welcome to the Jungle* vibrated the building and the air around it.

When I was ten feet away, the door burst open and Hondo staggered out with two feet of slim, shining blade protruding from his chest. I caught Hondo as he fell and saw the silver hilt of the sword cane hard against his back, like a pushpin stuck into cardboard.

There was commotion and angry yells growing louder from the darkness of the doorway. Music throbbed the air as Axl scream-sang, *"Welcome to the jungle, welcome to the...nah-nah nah-nah nah-nah naaah..."* I pulled my magnum and pointed it at the door as I put the other arm around Hondo's chest and drug him to my truck.

A man appeared, the one whose eyes I had soaped, and he raised his pistol. I fired three fast shots and he yelped and fell back into the dark. I felt behind me, found the door handle and opened the passenger door.

Hondo said, "I can make it." I don't know how, but he stood on his feet and pulled himself into the cab. I kept the magnum on the door and went to the driver's side, got in and started the engine.

When we started moving, several others came out of the door and one had a shotgun. I snapped off two shots and made them duck, but they fired from hunched positions and I heard the buckshot and bullets thunk into the side of the truck. I whipped the wheel and squealed through the other cars and was on the road headed for the hospital before they fired another shot.

CHAPTER TEN

Hondo groaned. He used an index finger to touch the needle-sharp point of the sword, whispering in a pain-filled voice, "Sticky situation."

The guy is making jokes. "Can't leave you alone for a minute," I said. "So what happened, was there a sign on the door saying, 'Free Shishkebab' and you just had to have some?" I glanced at him as I snaked through the heavy traffic. Flecks of bright blood dappled his lips.

"You're...you're like a thorn in my side." Hondo said.

The traffic slowed to a stall and I could see the dust from a collision maybe two hundred yards ahead. I turned the wheel and drove Shamu over the curb and into a strip mall lot and powered over curbs, across streets and over landscaped areas where I demolished a dozen small trees and shrubs. The hospital was four blocks away, so I continued overland. At the end of another strip mall, I roared over the curb, crossed a side street, and then slid into a paint store parking lot.

I glanced at Hondo and his head rested against the window, his eyes closed. A long mound of dirt and gravel blocked the way to the hospital. I glanced at the highway. Still no movement. A construction crew readied to rebuild the side road, and safety signs lined the top of the mounds and on both ends. Men in hard hats waited for heavy machinery to do their magic.

"This might be bumpy," I said to Hondo, but he didn't hear. I put Shamu in four-wheel drive, held Hondo's shoulder and drove over the ten-foot high mound as men yelled at me from both sides.

I crossed several more store parking lots and then raced across manicured grass to the hospital. As I pulled into the

Emergency Entrance, Hondo touched my arm. "Accident," he said.

"You sure?"

"No police. Fell on it..." and he passed out again.

The people in emergency are fast and good. They looked at me when I said it was an accident, but they focused on their patient and ignored my story.

I called Hunter and sat in the waiting room. She came down the hall and sat by me. A half dozen other people waiting on injured loved ones waited in chairs and leaned against the wall.

"How is he?" Hunter asked.

I shrugged. "Don't know. He was coherent when we got here."

"The Doctor hasn't talked to you?"

"Not yet. They're still with him." Hunter reached for my hand and held it as we sat and listened to the sounds that trickled out of ER into the waiting room.

**

It was another hour before a young doctor came out to talk to us. He said, "Your friend is going to make it."

I took a deep breath and let it out. Hunter hugged my arm.

The Doctor said, "One lung collapsed and the blade scraped the outside of the heart, but didn't puncture it. The sword was wedged so tight we had to go in and pry the ribs apart before we could remove it." He was agitated and had more to say, so we waited. "Your friend is very tough, even telling us before he was sedated that he fell on the sword, but...and here is where I'm having problems, there was evidence that the sword had been yanked back and forth several times, like someone trying to dislodge it. Would that have been you?"

"Not me, Doctor. I got there after he'd fallen. He told me the handle hung in a banister when he fell and he'd pulled against it trying to get loose."

The doctor mulled that over. "He'll be in recovery for another hour, then we'll put him in a room. You can visit him then." He paused, "Your friend is...very in control. Most people go into shock, but his pulse and respiration remained steady. Was he by chance in the military?" I nodded. He continued, "I thought maybe that was it. Lots of signs of violence on that young man's body."

I didn't elaborate.

The Doctor said, "He also said he wanted the sword with him after he woke up and to tell you, let me get this right, 'We'll have a pointed conversation' when he wakes up. I assume that is a joke."

I nodded. "Always the kidder."

"The sword in his room is something we can't allow."

"I'll tell him."

The doctor nodded, then went back through the doors and we went to the cafeteria to drink some coffee until Hondo was in his room.

Hunter said, "Found out a few things."

I'd been thinking of Hondo, but said, "Like what?"

"For one, Bond Savitch was a Russian citizen who immigrated as a child twenty years ago and became a naturalized US citizen eleven years ago. She came over with her parents and lived as a LAPR" --she pronounced it *lap-er* -- "until she had the required residency to naturalize."

"What's a LAPR?"

"Lawfully Admitted Permanent Resident. It's Immigration terminology."

"Anything else?"

"Uh-huh. Our friend Mr. Rakes was an officer in the Spetsnaz, the Soviet Special Forces, before he was sent to prison."

"Did it say what charge?"

"He was jailed as a political prisoner, is what I read."

"That's the last thing I'd have thought."

"Me too. Some of our records from former Soviet countries are a little, ahh, cloudy. It was all they had to go with his application though, so he was allowed in after being released from prison and pardoned by the Russian government. He's a LAPR, too."

"Did you happen to look up Simon Mortay?"

"No, but I can tomorrow."

"Thanks." I could still see Mortay with his sword cane the day Hondo faced him down.

A nurse came over to tell us Hondo was in his room and we went up.

**

Hondo's chest was bandaged and there was a drain tube leading out of the gauze to a soft plastic bag attached to the bottom of his bed frame. There was watery pink fluid dripping into it. An IV drip was going in his left arm. He looked sleepy and had dark hollows under his eyes, but he was awake.

I pointed to the drain bag below his bed. "They going to run that back through?"

Hondo said, "One can only hope."

Hunter moved beside him and brushed the hair from his forehead. "You've probably felt better, huh?"

Hondo nodded. I said, "They won't allow you to have the sword in here."

He shrugged, "I thought it was worth a try."

I said, "You feel up to telling us about it?"

He nodded and told us what happened.

**

Hondo parked off-center behind a suburban, thirty yards from the entrance to the Caspian Diamond. He left his driver's view open to the front door, with the rest of the Mercedes hidden behind the big Chevy. He wore his sunglasses and listened to a CD of

Motown's Greatest Hits, observing those who came and went through the smoked glass door and into the darkness beyond. Each time the door opened music escaped and over the next thirty minutes, Hondo heard clipped refrains from various artists ranging from Eminem to Aerosmith to Adele.

    A Lexus pulled into the parking lot behind him and Hondo watched in his rear view mirror as a petite strawberry blond Hispanic woman got out and walked to the door. She wore tight designer jeans, Reeboks and a tucked-in white tee shirt. The small red purse hung at her hip from a thin strap that ran over the shoulder.

    She opened the door and Hondo heard Katy Perry singing California Gurls as the woman disappeared into the dark. The song went silent as the door closed. Hondo replaced the Motown CD with the Stones and adjusted the volume down. He thought about calling Ronny, but figured he'd wait.

    A *thump* came from the entrance door. Hondo watched, and several seconds later the door burst open to Katy singing and the small strawberry haired woman running out screaming, her tee shirt half torn off and fluttering behind her. Carl Rakes was several steps behind but caught up fast and yanked her backward by the hair. The woman fell and screamed. Carl wrapped her under one arm and walked back inside. It all happened in less than twenty seconds.

    Hondo took off his glasses, put them on the dash and trotted toward the doors. A large bald headed man wearing a black leather jacket came out and held his hand up for Hondo to stop. Someone inside turned up the volume to ear-splitting levels and Axl Rose vibrated the outside air with, *Welcome to the Jungle*.

    The man at the door was good. Hondo pulled his Glock and the man leaped at him, grabbing the pistol with both hands. He hit the magazine release and it dropped from the pistol.

Hondo fired the remaining round into the man's shoulder and the man grunted and kicked the magazine into the parking lot. Hondo dropped the Glock and hit him with a three-punch combination. The man crashed into the wall, then sunk to the ground, head lolling.

Hondo opened the smoked glass door and walked into darkness and the ear-throbbing music. Carl had the woman at the edge of the bar near the office door. Rakes held her hair with one hand and slapped her hard across the face with the other. "Vhere de Veemin? Vhere de shid Veemin?" The woman had her arms up, but Carl's blows were knocking them away like they were nothing.

Carl saw Hondo and snarled orders at two rough looking men. They came at Hondo with their fists clenched. Hondo kicked the first one hard in the face and he went sprawling across the floor. The second one swung a roundhouse at Hondo's head and Hondo blocked it, then grabbed the man by his throat and crotch, lifted him and threw him into a cluster of tables and chairs. The man landed hard and didn't get up.

Carl released the tiny woman, who staggered away, regained her senses and ran by Hondo and out the door. A naked dancer and the rest of the crowed moved as far away as they could get.

Carl moved to his left as Hondo walked toward him. Rakes circled until Hondo was standing at the edge of the bar, his back to the office door. The air throbbed with the music.

Carl yelled to be heard, "Voman is gone. Is over. You go now."

Hondo said, "Not yet."

Carl smiled, "You wish for the hurt from me, Dah? I break your shidsnarl face and piss at your throad."

Hondo was concentrating on Rakes when he felt the smallest push of air from behind him. *Door*, Hondo thought and started to turn as a lightning bolt hit him in the back and rocketed molten-hot pain completely through his chest.

Hondo went down on his side with a weight riding him to the floor. Simon Mortay was on him, his hand still on the sword cane's hilt.

Hondo tried to breath and the pain was terrible, like an exposed nerve in a tooth being scraped with a file. He struggled and heard Carl laugh. The weight came off his back and Simon stood up, then put his foot against Hondo's back and tried to pull out the sword, but it wouldn't come. Mortay pulled several times, yanking hard enough to drag Hondo's body several feet.

Carl said, "I pull it," and took a step toward them.

Hondo pushed with his legs and one arm and got to his feet. He pulled the Black Ops knife from his pocket, opened it with the same move and continued the motion with the blade toward Carl's throat.

Carl's eyes widened and he jerked back. The blade left a tiny red line across the front of his adam's apple. Mortay yelled and jumped away and he and Carl watched Hondo stagger, holding the knife out toward them, ready to do battle.

Mortay's eyes flickered to the side and Hondo turned to see one of the men against the wall raising a pistol. Hondo threw the knife and it buried to the hilt in the man's shoulder. He screamed and the pistol clattered at his feet. The baldheaded man staggered inside and went behind the bar, reaching for something below the cash register.

Hondo ran for the doors and burst into daylight.

**

"And that's where Ronny caught me as I fell," Hondo said.

"Jesus," Hunter said.

"It was my fault," Hondo said. "I wanted Rakes so bad I got careless."

I said, "You're lucky Mortay likes the blade. If he favored pistols you might not be here."

"Oh yeah, I feel real lucky. But you're right."

"Course I'm right. World's Most Infallible Investigator."

"Most Phallic Investigator, is that what you said?" Hunter said.

"Hey, that's not nice."

Hondo started to smile, then coughed and we saw the pain go through him. He said, "Don't make me laugh."

"Us?" I said, "Hey, at least we're not like Carl Rakes and are gonna piss at your throat. Can you imagine if that guy wrote a dictionary, how the words would look? Or worse, what if he did commercials? Think about him explaining Preparation H. Guy would be unbelievable."

Hondo coughed and held up a hand in surrender. A nurse came in and went to him, looking concerned. She said, "You are aggravating him, and he's been severely injured."

I said, "Probably needs a chuckle-ectomy." Hondo coughed.

The nurse shooed us from his room. No sense of humor, those nurses.

**

I started up Shamu as Hunter said, "Don't go do anything crazy."

"Me? What about you, the female version of Dirty Harry?"

"I'm just saying, we need to do this with cool heads, not let emotion rule."

I said, "And we still haven't found Bob Landman, who's in big trouble for sure."

"Right. So let's cool down, figure our next move."

"Sure," I said. "I need to do one thing first. I'll drop you at the office, then be back in an hour."

Hunter looked at me, "Ronny..."

"Scout's honor," I said. "I'm not going after Rakes or Mortay."

I dropped Hunter off and headed for Siberia on Sunset. I went inside and Frank Meadows was holding court on the couches with several younger exec types in casual Armani and wearing Rolexes on their tanned wrists.

Frank said to them, "The real hidden talent is fiscal management. Like I demand at Americas, we know where every penny is going, and where it comes from. Makes all the difference during those lean times between blockbusters."

I walked up, "And you'd know all about those lean times, wouldn't you, Frank. What is it, Americas Studios had produced the four biggest flops in the last five years, that about right?"

Frank's right eye twitched as he looked at me, "Baca, this is a private conversation."

"Why don't you tell them how you funnel money made from criminal enterprise into your studio so you can keep it afloat?"

One of the men got up and said, "I'll talk to you later, Mr. Meadows." The others left with him and I sat down beside Frank.

He started to get up and I snugged his elbow into the crook of my arm and used my hand to force his hand down at a right angle. A little more pressure and I could inflict a lot of pain. A little more than that and I could break his wrist.

"Frank, tell me about Carl Rakes." Frank tried a quick move to pull his hand away and punch me, but I applied the pressure and he grimaced. I said, "You try that again and I'll break your wrist so bad that hand will fly around on the end of your arm like a propeller. Now, tell me about Rakes."

He growled, "What do you want to know?"

"How'd you meet him?"

He looked at me like he thought I already knew, "Bond introduced us."

"Bond?"

"Yeah, I thought she told you."

"Nope." I thought a moment then said, "It doesn't bother you, Bond rubbing all over him?"

"You really that naive, Baca?"

"Answer the question."

"Carl is both our partners."

"I'm not talking about business. I saw what was going on at the pool."

"That's what I'm talking about. Both Bond and I are omnisexual."

"So plants and animals are fair game, too."

Frank rolled his eyes, "We have sex together."

"They used to call it *ménage a trois*."

"You common people have such small minds."

"Common people? Frank, I hear a lot of Pennsylvania coal mine in your voice. Doesn't get more common than that."

Frank struggled and I gave his wrist a good one that brought a hiss from his lips. He settled back, not wanting that kind of pain again. We stared at each other for a minute, then he said, "What I know, Carl Rakes was in the Russian Special Forces and sided with the wrong group during one of the Russian political changeovers. The victors thought he was too dangerous so they arrested him for crimes against the state and stuck him in jail. Not just any jail, but the one filled with the meanest, sickest, toughest criminals in the country, the prison at Sarana.

He was forced to become the toughest one there just to survive. Seems convicts have a thing for military or police when they join the prison population. Anyhow, that's what he did.

"What goes around comes around, and some of his political cronies came back into power years later and they freed and pardoned him. He'd had enough of Mother Russia and he immigrated to America about seven years ago. We met and I hired him. That what you wanted?"

"How did Bond know him before you?"

"I don't know. Ask her."

Frank sulled up and I figured that was all I was going to get, so I let him go. He rubbed his wrist and said, "You keep sticking your nose where it doesn't belong and you're going to get hurt."

I moved my face close to his, "Simon Mortay ran my best friend through with a sword. I think Rakes beat Mickey Haile to death with his fists. I'm not the one who needs to watch out. Tell them that." I walked to the bar and ordered a Tunguska Blast. I needed it after that little episode. I watched Frank in the mirror behind the bar as I downed the Blast. The combination of hot/cold secret ingredients, and one hundred proof octane blossomed in my stomach and spread outward like the pressure waves on those old films of exploding nuclear bombs. When I left, my fingers, toes, and scalp were tingling as if they'd been massaged with menthol. I didn't know what was in that stuff, but it was worth the twenty bucks.

**

When I got to the office, Hunter was waiting. She was mad clear through, but not at me.

"Somebody's got a long reach, Ronny. I got a call from my Chief a few minutes ago, seems I'm to report directly to Washington to face a review board on my conduct."

"What are they saying you did?"

"Worked out here with you and Hondo without getting prior authorization."

I'll tell them you were just tagging along. I mean, we didn't pay you, so you weren't really working."

She shook her head, "Whoever did this has some juice, because they're going hard at me, is what the Chief said. It's a firing offense."

"So what are you going to do?"

"I've got a flight out in three hours. I'm going by to see Hondo, then head for the airport. I'm sorry to leave you like this, but..."

"Hey, you do what you need to. If I can testify or anything, tell them they're wrong, let me know or have them call me."

She nodded, walked over, gave me a hug, and left before we both got emotional.

The office felt empty. Hondo was in the hospital and I'd gotten used to Hunter being here. Right then, if I'd had ten of those Tunguska Blasts I'd have popped them all down. I walked to the windows and looked at the full parking lot. Several people in gym clothes were beside Shamu looking at the bullet holes. One girl put her finger in the holes.

I looked past them and saw a Sheriff's Department sedan pull into the lot. Vick Best got out and walked toward my office. When he was close, I opened the door. "Hello Vick."

He walked past me into the office and plopped in a chair. He rubbed his head and sighed.

I closed the door and sat behind my desk. "Spit it out," I said.

"Your Investigator's license has been suspended. You're no longer authorized to do private investigations in the state of California."

"Suspended for what?"

"Ronny, it came down from high up, is all I can tell you. Some sort of ethics violation. They're going to review it, give you a chance to respond, then make a final decision, but until then, you're suspended."

"Hondo too?" Vick nodded.

"You know who?"

"No."

We sat there in silence, then Vick said, "Your permit to carry is suspended, too."

I nodded. It figured.

He rose and put his hand on my shoulder, "It comes to it, I'll testify in your behalf."

"Thanks."

"I gotta go, tell Hondo he's in our thoughts."

"I will." Vick left and closed the door behind him.

What a day, I thought. I took off my shoulder holster and magnum and hung it in the closet, then moped around the office for the next hour but didn't accomplish anything so I drove to the auto body shop and the body man came out, cleaning his hands on a red rag.

"Christ, Baca. You tell them where to shoot so they'd hit the only place hasn't been repaired before? I'm gonna buy stock in Bond-O before I start this one. Price'll go through the roof. Leave it and I'll get to it soon."

"You got a loaner?"

"Sure, take that one," He pointed at a five year old mint green Yugo. It looked like something from Toys R Us. "Keys are in it," he said.

"Do I wind it up or does it take batteries?"

"Ha-ha, funny guy. Gets a gazillion miles a gallon, so you won't spend a fortune driving it this week."

"It's going to take a week to fix my truck?"

"I got others before you. I'll work on it between other jobs. It's the best I can do."

"All right," I said. "Call me if you finish it sooner."

"Oh sure, Captain Ahab."

"Very funny."

"Not every guy in town drives a fish-mobile."

"It's not...never mind." I went to the Yugo and folded myself inside like an accordion. It was actually roomier that I thought it would be. I started it up and we putted our way to the hospital.

**

I parked and rode the elevator to the third floor and walked to Hondo's room. The door was closed and I started to push it open, but a nurse stopped me. "You can't go in there. He's not allowed visitors."

"I just saw him not six hours ago," I said.

"Are you Mr. Baca?"

"Yes."

"Before he lost consciousness."

"What?"

"He's very ill, Mr. Baca. He said to tell you the little dancer came to visit and you need to find her."

"How's he ill? What happened?"

"Pneumonia."

"But, it's so fast."

She said, "Some people call it Galloping Pneumonia, but the technical name is Streptococcus Pneumonia Group A. It's bacterial." She touched my forearm, "Do you remember the Muppet fellow who passed away?"

"Jim Henson, sure."

"He died of streptococcus pneumonia less than twenty hours after being admitted to the hospital. It's a very fast-acting strain, resistant to many antibiotics. This is the type your friend has."

I felt all the strength go out of me. "Will he make it?"

"I don't know. We're doing everything we can, and he is in phenomenal shape. We'll know more tomorrow."

"Can I look in on him?"

She bit her lip then said, "For a moment, no more."

I went in and saw Hondo under an oxygen tent. He looked flushed and was having trouble breathing. His eyes were closed and his arms were under the clear tent. I watched him for a minute, then said, "You make it or I'm going to be pissed." I wiped my eyes and left the room.

The nurse was waiting outside and I said, "Will you call me if there's any change?"

"Yes, we have your number."

I left the hospital in a daze. The sun was disappearing beyond the sea. I turned on the Yugo's lights after taking several minutes figuring out which knob and button went to what. Hondo's message said, The little dancer, and I assumed he meant the one he'd rescued at the Caspian Diamond. Finding her might be a chore since I didn't know her name or address, and I'd be less than welcome at the Diamond.

I thought about it as I drove up Mulholland and took the road to my house, then saw an orange glow in the sky.

The fire trucks beat me there. My house was blazing away like a high school bonfire. I parked the Yugo and stepped out to stare. The roof collapsed in a plume of sparks and embers rising on the smoke.

I sat on the curb and for some reason an old interview with Willie Nelson popped in my head where Willie told of the day his record company fired him, his third wife served divorce papers, and he came home to see his house burning to the ground. Willie sat on the curb and wrote, *What Can You Do To Me Now*.

Great, now I was living a country song.

CHAPTER ELEVEN

I watched the house burn to a pile of rubble and when the fire department left, I followed them down Mulholland and took the road to the hospital. If they wouldn't let me stay in the room with Hondo I'd stay in the visitor's area. At least it had a couch.

I tried five times to see him. The first four I tried Sneaky. I'd wait until the nurses were all busy and I would creep to Hondo's door, and each time I was caught before I could enter. The fifth time I tried Clever. I was in the cafeteria when I saw a male doctor leave his white lab coat on the back of his chair. I knew the next shift of nurses were on and none of them had caught me. The idea blossomed. I put on the lab coat and went to the nurses' station. I told them I was a lung specialist and needed to check on Mr. Wells. The nurses looked at each other, then back at me. The one closest to me, the redhead, folded her arms on her chest and said, "Okay Doctor, would you like us to perform percutaneous radiofrequency trigeminal ganglioysis?"

A trickle of sweat ran down my temple. I said, "Of course, I'll need you to do that."

"And where would you like that administered on Mr. Wells?"

I felt like the proverbial deer in the headlights. "Let's go in rectally."

That brought a snort, then laughter and head shaking from all of them. The redhead said, "That procedure is performed behind the eye. Please sit down, Mr. Baca. We'll let you in when we can." To top it off, they asked me for the lab coat. I went to the waiting room and tried to close my eyes. Every hour, I opened them and saw that ten minutes had passed. Dawn took forever to arrive.

At seven-thirty, the nurse that had taken my lab coat came and tapped me on the shoulder, "Come with me," she said.

A cold knot formed in my stomach. I followed her to the nurses' station and she said, "Mr. Wells made it through the night and that's a good sign. He's still not out of danger, and he's still unconscious, but if you want to go in there and sit with him, I'll let you."

I went in and looked at Hondo through the plastic oxygen tent. He looked like he'd lost twenty pounds and his face was pale. I went to the bed and touched his arm through the plastic. "I'm right here," I said. I moved a chair closer to the bed and tried to think optimistic thoughts.

Two hours later, as I watched the television, I heard a weak voice say, "Find Landman." Hondo's eyes were open.

"Hey," I said.

Hondo cleared his throat and said again, "Landman, go find him."

"I think I'll hang out with you instead."

He shook his head slowly and coughed, "No, get to work. Make us some money."

"We're not getting paid for this one, remember?"

"Do it for Sparta."

"Uh-huh."

"I'm fine. You make me nervous, all hovering like you are. Go do Good Guy stuff."

"I'll go as soon as I know you're all right."

"Look at me, I'm *not* all right. I've got a hole through me and my lungs feel like they're full of hot glue. It's hard to breathe, but I'm not going to die. I'm going to get well, but not soon enough to help you do what you need to do."

A nurse who looked to be in her late forties came in and checked Hondo's vital signs. She smiled after taking his temperature and said, "Your fever's going down. That is excellent, young man."

After the nurse left I said, "I guess I could go do something. No sense hanging around here to watch you sleep. Did you know you make baby noises when you go night-night?"

"Only when I've been skewered."

"Uh-huh." I stood and said, "I'm off to do some top-flight detective work. Don't forget to eat your hospital food."

Hondo said, "Yum." He coughed again and looked at me with fever-bright eyes, "Find Landman. I'll deal with Rakes and Mortay when I get out of here."

"Sure," I said, "By the time the hospital discharges you, both of them will be dead from old age. Good plan."

"You're so witty," Hondo said, then his brow wrinkled, "Mickey's funeral is today, right?"

I nodded, "Yeah, at one."

"Tell her parents I'm sorry I can't be there."

"I will."

**

I drove the Yugo to the office where I showered and shaved. I didn't have a suit, but there was a Men's Wearhouse not too far away so I drove there and bought a dark blue suit with white shirt and dark blue tie. That made one suit, two pairs of jeans, one black polo short sleeve shirt, six pairs of socks and underwear, four tee shirts and four pairs of athletic shorts. I had one other piece of clothing and was taking it with me to the funeral. The rest of my clothes were all ash-black and blowing across the California landscape with every breeze. I didn't find any shoes that felt good, so I wore my New Balance shoes with the suit.

The funeral was at graveside, and only a small group of about a dozen people attended. The casket was closed because of the beating Mickey had taken, but I asked the funeral director if I might place something inside the casket.

"I'll open it for you," he said. I followed him to the casket and waited until he opened it about six inches. I took my Patagonia windbreaker and placed it beside her. The director nodded, then closed the casket.

I recognized Mickey's parents right away. They were small framed like Mickey, and the woman had Mickey's eyes. The pastor gave a nice eulogy, and he kept it short, not pretending he knew Mickey Haile well. Afterwards I walked by the parents and told them Hondo was ill and couldn't make it, but that we were sorry for their loss.

The father looked at me a moment and said, "Are you Ronny Baca?"

"Yes."

He rose and said, "Please walk with me." I followed him as we moved away from the crowd. He stopped about thirty yards away and turned. I could see grief etched deep into his face. He said, "Mickey was very taken with you."

"I liked her, too."

A tiny smile touched his lips when I said 'her'. He continued, "She thought you could do anything, and she was so proud to have you and Mr. Wells as friends."

"I'm going to find the people who hurt her, Mr. Haile."

He appraised me. "I believe you will, Mr. Baca." He sighed and looked to his wife at the grave site. "I should get back with Mary. Please tell Mr. Wells we wish him a fast recovery." He walked to his wife and I got into the Yugo, where I sat for several minutes before driving to the office.

**

I changed into jeans and a blue tee shirt, then went through the mutual door of our office and Archie's gym. I saw Arch coaching one of the Raiders through a leg workout on the extension machine. I recognized him as one of the corners on the Raiders' defense who lived in Los Angeles in the off season. He was one of those hard-hitting defensive backs that receivers said should have to wear red lights and sirens on their helmets to warn people when they were coming. I remembered he was out last season with a knee injury.

Archie said to him, "I talked to your surgeon yesterday and we worked out a next-level program for you. It's pretty easy."

The Pro's bald, ebony head was already beaded with sweat. He said, "Arch, you think building the pyramids is easy."

I reached them and said to the D back, "You mind if I talk to Arch for a minute?"

"Please. It'll give me a break."

Arch wasn't going to let it go that easy. He said, "Start with this: three sets of descending reps, twenty-five, twenty, and fifteen, using the same weight. Alternate one leg, then the other and don't rest between sets, then go to the leg curl machine and do it again for the leg biceps. I want you to work up to using one-fifty on this one."

"What weight do you want me to start with?"

"Oh, about one-forty-five." The guy's eyes widened and I saw Arch slap his thigh and say, "Haw! Just start with less than you think you can lift. Finishing all the reps is what's most important, building your groove and setting the muscles up for what'll be coming."

We left him putting on plates and I said, "I need to use your phone."

"You don't have one in your office?"

"If who I phone has caller ID, I don't want it to show up for the office."

He pointed toward his office, "It's in there. Close the door if you want." He paused and said, "How's Hondo? I figure you being here means he's better."

"Yeah, better but weak. He developed pneumonia. Almost didn't make it through the night."

Archie shook his head, "You need anything..." I nodded. He said, "Tell Hondo to get well, the power lifters want another shot at him on the bench press." He patted me on the shoulder with affection, and it clicked my teeth together. Tough love.

I called the Caspian Diamond and said in my best redneck voice, "That little red-headed Mexican dancer y'all got gonna be dancing' tonight?"

The voice said, "I'm sorry, Blanca doesn't perform here anymore."

"Oh yeah? What other club'd she go to?"

"I wouldn't know that."

"What was her last name anyway, case I see it somewhere at one a those other men's clubs."

"We don't give out that information."

"Okey-doke, then. Thankee." I hung up. I had her first name, now to get the rest.

I knew the green Lexus Blanca drove and could go to Vick and get him to eventually run it down through DMV, but then there would be a ton of questions and I wasn't sure I wanted to spill everything right then. I decided to unleash my secret weapon.

**

I walked into the empty lobby of the Camino Real and saw Loomis alone behind the reception desk. He recognized me and was looking somewhere between me and the wall when he winked in acknowledgment.

"Hey, Loomis. How's it going?"

"Pretty good. Had some Venusians check in this morning, in case you want some pictures."

"Venusians, huh?"

"Oh sure, I recognized 'em right off. They have all that pale blond hair and those icy blue eyes. It's a sure give-away, just like your paper showed in last October's issue. Did you write that one?"

"No, it was another reporter." I leaned my forearms on the counter, "Where are these Venusians saying they're from?"

Loomis snorted, "Some made-up place, here let me look." He punched some keys on the computer and said, "Here it is. Reykjavik. Like there's a place named that."

"Way to stay on your toes, Loomis." I leaned closer, "Say, you get a lunch break around here?"

"Sure. It starts in about a half hour."

"Can you go out to eat?"

"Yeah, but I brought a sandwich today."

"Thing is," I said in a low voice, "I need a little help on a case."

"I thought that was just your cover."

"It is, but to make it look legitimate we have to work a real case every once in a while."

"Oh, sure. I knew that."

"What I need is someone smart like you to go into a place and ask a few questions. I can't go because they know me inside. You think you could help?"

"Well..."

"Loomis, you'd have to go to a gentlemen's club and look at nude dancers and ask a few questions. I'll give you money to spend and give you a hundred dollars to put in your pocket. What do you say?"

"These are naked women, right?"

"Beautiful women, Loomis."

"I'll come out in thirty minutes."

"That's my man," I said.

Loomis cleaned up before leaving the hotel. I wasn't sure it was an improvement. He wore a red plaid polyester jacket, and he used so much gel on his hair it looked like he'd just stepped out of a shower and hadn't dried his head.

He hopped in the Yugo and said, "Boy, nobody'd figure you for a detective in this thing, huh?" I opened the glove box and got out the small ear pieces and lapel microphones that I brought from the office.

"We'll use these to communicate while you're inside and I'm outside." Loomis nodded, his eyes fixed on them. I took an earpiece and fitted it to him. My fingers came in contact with the hair above his ears and were instantly slippery. I looked out the side window past Loomis and said, "Hey, is that Elvis?"

Loomis twisted around to look and I wiped my hands on the back of his plaid jacket. "Nahh," I said, "Don't guess it was the King." Loomis turned to face me and I put the lapel mike on his shirt, making sure to put it where the jacket wouldn't rub across the face of the mike and make loud scratching noises in my ear. When I was satisfied, I filled him in on what I wanted him to say, gave him three hundred dollars and a plain manila envelope to keep in his jacket pocket. "You ready?" I asked.

"I've never seen a live naked woman," he said. "I can hardly wait."

**

I parked behind a Lincoln near the Caspian Diamond's entrance and went over it one more time with Loomis, who was itching to get out the door. "I'll be able to hear everything you say and everything said to you. I can talk to you through the earpiece so we can communicate just like we are now."

"I got it. I'm ready."

"Okay, go get 'em," I said.

I could hear Loomis breathing as he walked inside. Jennifer Lopez was singing her newest song and I could hear the occasional clinks of glasses and other muted sounds. After several seconds the music sounded the same. "Loomis, are you standing?"

"Uh, yeah. She's beautiful."

"Find a table by the stage so you can talk to the women when they go up to dance."

I heard some shuffling and the sound of something bumping, then a voice said, "Watch where you're going. You can stare at the girls after you sit down."

Loomis mumbled an apology and I heard him sit down. A waitress came over and he ordered a drink. A Zombie. When the song ended Loomis hissed, "She's coming this way!"

"Just do like we planned." I rubbed my forehead.

I heard Loomis say, "Uhh, hey."

A woman's voice said, "Hi, did you enjoy the performance?"

"Oh yeah," Loomis sounded excited, "Do you practice on a pole like that or is it just something natural?"

"I practice."

The waitress brought the Zombie and I heard Loomis gulp three or four times and say, "I'll have another one, and could you bring something for the lady?"

The woman ordered a Seven and Seven. Loomis said, "You cold? I ask cause your nipples are real hard. Mine get like that when I rub ice cubes on them."

"Loomis!" I said into the mike.

I heard a clatter, then the woman said, "Did something bite you?"

Loomis said, "Uhh..."

"Tell her it's an old war wound that acts up."

He told her and I heard the waitress return and put down their drinks. I heard Loomis glug three times and say, "I'll take another one."

I said, "Loomis, slow down. You don't have anything on your stomach." I didn't hear anything back. I continued, "Ask her like we rehearsed."

Loomis did pretty well, considering he drank four more Zombies in the next five minutes. He told the woman he was looking for a dancer named Blanca, but didn't know her last name. The woman said Blanca didn't work at the Diamond anymore. Loomis said he was to deliver a package to Blanca from an admirer who used to watch her dance, but was dying and wanted to give her this little token of his appreciation. He said it was too bad Blanca wasn't working here, but did the woman know where she was? Loomis showed the woman the manila envelope with ten one hundred dollar bills, then told her if she could get him to Blanca, she would get a reward. The woman hesitated and Loomis placed a hundred dollars on the table and told her she could have that if she knew where he could find Blanca. He told her there would be another hundred if he found Blanca.

The woman took the hundred and told him an address in Culver City.

**

Loomis threw up in the Yugo before we returned to the Camino Real. He apologized and was going to take off his jacket to use as a rag when I told him I'd take care of it. My eyes watered. I rolled down the window and turned my nose to the wind.

"Why did you order Zombies?" I asked.

"The only drink name I knew."

"You could have ordered beer."

"I didn't think that's what people drank in naked clubs." He felt miserable and I didn't question him any more. When I let him out, I drove to the nearest car wash and spent three dollars in quarters cleaning out the passenger side. I paid a dollar for some kind of strawberry air freshener -- the only kind they had -- and placed it at Ground Zero. It helped a little.

The address in Culver City was in a Hispanic neighborhood. I got some long stares as I cruised in the Yugo, looking for the house number. I found it in the middle of the next block. The house was originally built in the forties and was well maintained with the yard neat and green. I parked at the curb and walked to the front door. A doorbell was by the knob and I pushed it, hearing the faint ring inside.

The door had three small, face high panes of glass descending like stairs across the door. I put my eye against one and could see through a thin curtain. A woman was getting out of a recliner. She put down a newspaper and walked to the door. I pulled my face back and the door opened. The Hispanic woman was probably in her fifties. She looked at me with a frown.

I said, "Miss, I'm looking for Blanca. Is she here?"

"*No hablo Ingles.*"

I could see the living room behind her. The newspaper was the Los Angeles Times, in English. There was a Redbook beside it and an old Bewitched rerun was on the television, with Elizabeth Montgomery and the rest of the actors speaking their lines in English. I said, "Blanca's in danger. I'm here to help her."

The woman didn't move or speak.

We had a silent face-off for thirty seconds, until she won. I sighed and said, "My friend is the one who helped her escape at the Caspian Diamond. He was almost killed doing it. I know Blanca went by to see him while he was in the hospital. Her enemies wouldn't know that." The woman didn't acknowledge I'd spoken. I said, "I'll go wait in the car for five minutes. If you don't put me in touch with Blanca by then, I'll drive off. But know this, those men are hunting her just like I am, and if I can find this address, so can they." I went to the Yugo, got in and tuned the radio to NPR, where they were describing the incredible distances whales could hear each other under water. After a couple of minutes, I figured if the human race could learn to talk in hoots, whistles, and clicks we could just stick our heads in the water and talk across the globe. Then again, being put on hold might result in a lot of drownings.

The door of the house opened and the woman stepped outside holding a cordless phone and beckoning me to her.

The woman said, "Blanca's on the line. She wants to talk to you."

"Wow," I said, "That *Learn to Speak English in Thirty Seconds* course from Rosetta Stone really works, huh?" She made a face like tasting something sour and handed me the phone.

I said, "Hello."

"You're his friend?"

"Yeah."

"Okay, tell me what room he's in."

"Three fifteen."

"Anybody could find that out with a call."

"Yeah they could, but nobody except someone he talked to would know you visited him. He told me you snuck past the nurses, and you thanked him for saving you. He almost died that night because of pneumonia, did you know that?"

"No, but he seemed to have trouble breathing when we talked."

"Hondo made it through the night and when he regained consciousness this morning, he told me to find you."

"How did you?"

"I'm a world famous super sleuth."

She ignored my comment. "You think Rakes or Mortay can track me to my aunt's place just like you?"

"You're lucky, your fellow performers at the club don't seem to be telling their bosses everything they know. I think you've got a little time, but eventually Rakes will find you." I could hear her breath shudder.

She said, "If we meet, how will I know you?"

"We've already met. I'm the one who asked you if you were from Durango."

"That's you?"

"Uh-huh. So where do you want to meet?"

Blanca said, "You know the Tar Pits?"

"Yep."

"I'll be there in an hour, by the entrance. I'll wait fifteen minutes and if you don't come, I'm going to Mexico."

"I'll be there." I heard a click and then handed the phone to the woman. "You think that Rosetta Stone course, *The One Minute Brain Surgeon*, would work for me?"

The woman said, "Somebody already operated on your crazy head, *pendejo*."

I walked to the car, sure my charm had won her over. *Pendejo* was probably the Spanish word for handsome.

**

I reached La Brea in forty minutes and saw Blanca standing by the entrance. I walked to her. "Looks like we're both early."

"I'm scared, this is too open here."

I pointed at the Yugo, "Let's get in and drive somewhere less vulnerable."

"You drive that thing?"

"Doing what I can for the environment. It gets a gazillion miles per gallon."

"So do roller blades."

I drove south on La Brea and turned east on Santa Monica, reached Vine and took it to Hollywood. I pulled into a parking building and drove us to the top level where I eased into a space and we looked out over the three-foot high retaining wall at

Hollywood and LA. It was as safe as I could make us on short notice.

"Now," I said. "How would you like to start?"

"It's a long story."

"I've got all the time you need."

Blanca looked out over the city, took a deep breath and let it out, "I started dancing at the Caspian Diamond a year and a half ago. Mortay ran the Diamond and Carl Rakes came in often. I think he owns part of it too, or is some kind of partner or something. After six months, they approached me and asked if I knew anyone who was good at smuggling people across the border. When they said that, I knew the phones at the Diamond were tapped, because I'd called some people about smuggling my sister and some cousins into the US. Since they knew anyway, I didn't deny it, so I set up a meeting for them. I told them I wanted my family brought too, and Simon agreed.

"Anyway, next month I hear the people I knew had vanished off the face of the earth, and Simon and Carl had other people of their own doing the smuggling. I guess, once they were taught the route, they didn't need anybody else doing it. My sister and cousins were still in Durango, too. They didn't bring them until much later."

I said, "Do you know what route they used?"

"No, only that they crossed east of San Diego through the hills and met a van that drove them to somewhere near LA."

When did your relatives come?"

"Less than two weeks ago."

"Where are they now?"

"I don't know."

"Does Rakes have them?"

"No, that's why he was hurting me, trying to find out if I knew where they were. That's when your friend rescued me."

"And you don't know where they are."

"No. The last time I heard from my sister was on a message she left on the answering machine. It said they were saved by the star and he was taking them somewhere safe. She said she would call me, but I haven't heard from her."

"Did you save the message?"

"Yes, and Carl got into my apartment and heard it. That's why he thought I knew where Maria was."

"The star, do you think Maria's talking about Bob Landman?"

"The actor? How would she know somebody famous like that?"

"It seems when Mr. Landman gets into a role, he gets into a role."

"Huh?"

"Landman's going to portray a Border Patrol Agent in an upcoming movie. They say he tries to live the part before playing it."

She thought a minute, then said, "Maybe it is. Maria mentioned something about a beautiful man they met. It might be Landman. He's very handsome."

"Why is Rakes after your sister?"

"For what they carried."

"Like what?"

"Maria told me that was how they paid for part of their journey. The smugglers gave them small items to carry and if stopped by the Immigration, to say it was theirs."

"Do you know what they were carrying?"

"Maria told me she had a golden egg covered in jewels and inside was a tiny wagon."

"A wagon?"

"Like in Cinderella, is what she said."

I glanced in my rear view mirror as a black suburban with dark tinted windows pulled in ten feet behind us. The driver got out. It was the Russian whose eyes I had soaped.

Simon Mortay exited the passenger's side, looking like he was nothing but bones under the black suit. Charon the ferryman, come to collect his toll. He wasn't carrying a cane; instead Mortay had a large Beretta in his gloved hand.

Blanca's eyes were big and she whispered, "Oh no, no, no..."

I grabbed her arm, "When I get their attention, start the car and get out of here." She nodded.

My pistol was at the office, and I patted my clothes for anything to use and found a hardness in my shirt pocket. I got out, armed with a box of Tic-Tacs.

CHAPTER TWELVE

I went to the back of the Yugo and blocked their view through the rear window. My calf touched the rear bumper and I felt the car move as Blanca slid to the driver's side. "You son of the bitch," Mortay said. "You vill get the same as your friend."

He was three feet from me, standing in front of one Suburban headlight. The second Russian was in front of the other. I was the point of the V in front of them.

I opened the Tic-Tacs, shook out a half-dozen, and put them in my mouth. Holding out the box to Mortay, I said, "Want some? They'll do wonders for your breath."

Mortay slapped the box from my hand and it landed near his driver. "Hey," I said, "There's no need for that." I moved toward the box, and when my face was within a foot of the driver I rolled my tongue into a tube, took a deep breath and shot the Tic-Tacs out of my mouth like a candy-dispensing machine gun. They hit the thug in the eyes and startled him. I grasped his arm, pulled him in front of me and ran him at Mortay as the Beretta came up and blossomed flame.

I heard the Yugo start and the tires squeal. Mortay paid no attention to the car and kept firing. The bullets struck the driver like hard slaps and I could feel him jerk with their impact. One passed through his body and hit me high in the chest.

It was like a large wasp stung me. When I felt the driver sag, I used my legs to heave him toward Simon, now pulling the trigger as fast as he could. The man fell into Mortay and knocked him backward several feet. I ducked and ran behind the Suburban for cover. I could hear the Yugo's engine whining as it sped down through the building.

Mortay yelled, "I kill you now!"

I dropped to look under the Suburban and watched his feet as he came around the front. I moved to the other side, then saw his hand and one knee come to the pavement.

The Suburban had a luggage rack on top, so I grabbed it and hopped to the roof, then rolled fast across and dropped on Simon as he rose.

I kicked his wrist as the Beretta came up and it went clattering across the pavement. Mortay spun with the kick and came to a standing position five feet from me. A long bladed knife glittered in his right hand.

He said, "I take your head to Carl. He vill reward me."

I was in my Bi-Jong stance when he came. I slapped his thrust aside and moved in, hitting him under the chin with the heel of my palm.

He went down but hung onto the knife. I stomped at his face and got a long slice along the edge of my lower leg for the trouble. I hopped back and Mortay rose as if pulled upright by a string.

I circled to my right, moving him until his back was to the low wall at the edge of the lot. I said, "This is for my friend," and went at him with a combination of strikes and feints with both fists and feet in an attack designed for each movement to take him a little farther off balance.

My last motion was a hard front kick to his chest, and I connected so well I felt the impact all the way through my hip. He was so skinny it was like kicking a bag of sticks.

Mortay tried to regain his balance but his legs hit the wall and he went over as his arms flailed the air.

I stepped to the wall and looked at the alley far below. Mortay lay with one leg under him and arms across his stomach. He could have been asleep except for the small red slick under his head.

I leaned against the Suburban and checked my chest. There was a large bruise where the bullet struck, but no penetration. I looked at my leg next. The blade broke the skin but was not deep. I went to the passenger door, opened it and sat in the seat, suddenly tired. Now that the adrenaline had stopped pumping through me, fatigue was setting in big-time. I could hear sirens in the distance and decided I would take a nap until they arrived.

**

After they finished questioning me and confirmed I was a good guy by talking to Vick Best, they let me go. As I left, I heard one of the police officers saying to another, "Guy was so cool he was sleeping when we got here."

If they only knew. The taxi got me to the office in good time and I could almost understand his heavily accented English as he tried to make conversation. I tipped him and went to the office. I called the hospital to check on Hondo. The nurse said he was asleep, but doing well. The doctors had downgraded him to guarded. I thanked her, hung up, then called Hunter on her cell phone.

She answered on the first ring, "Hello."

"How's it going?"

"Hey, Ronny. They've decided to hold off on the hearing until next week."

"Good, why don't you fly back here. I'll pick you up at the airport."

"Can't," she said, "They decided to detail me to DC, keep an eye on me. They have me working in Headquarters until the trial. At least while I'm up here I can look a little deeper into Rakes and Mortay." She changed the subject, "How's Hondo?"

"I just talked to the nurses. He's been downgraded to guarded."

"That is good news. How are you holding up?"

"Hanging in there."
"Is something wrong?"
"Nahh."
"What is it?"
"Nothing, nothing at all."
"Ronny Baca, you better tell me or I'm going to get mad."
I rubbed my forehead and said, "Mortay's dead."
There was a moment's silence, "Did you shoot him?"
"No."
"What happened?"
"Well, I had these Tic-Tacs…"

**

I hung up after another ten minutes with Hunter and went to the bathroom. Before I could finish, the phone rang. I hurried to zip up, then grabbed a paper towel, trotted over and picked up the receiver.

"Ronny Baca, waterproof private investigator."

"Baca is dirt under leg of dog."

"Hey Rakes, nice of you to have Simon drop in. Get it, drop in?"

"You make big mistake. I protect people who vork for me."

"You did a bang-up job with Ichabod Crane there. Looked like he thought he was a seagull the way he flapped his arms when I sent him off the roof." I actually heard Rakes growl.

"The days are numbering for you and friends. Sissy boy in hospital three five-teen room vill be easy, and you, and voman in Vashingtown."

"Talk's cheap."

"Is not talk."

"What do you think you're doing then, miming? Words are coming out of your mouth. That means you're talking. Is it too hard for your pea brain to digest?"

"Remember vhat I say. Your nose belongs some other place. You leave the veemin alone, or same happenings to you as boy-girl Meekee."

My grip tightened on the phone but I kept my cool, "How about if I just put my nose in what the women brought across the border? How about that?"

"Is not to bother the veemin! Stay away for dem. I varn you to go in other direction or you die from my hand."

"There you go again, yabbering like a parrot. Rakes want a cracker? Awwkk!"

"I ged you!" Rakes slammed down the receiver.

Boy, some people. But it worked and got me more information, because he was mad than I would get any other way.

Mortay worked for Rakes. That was interesting. Rakes deliberately let appearances indicate he was the subordinate, rather than Mortay. Rakes was smarter than I thought. He also knew what room Hondo was in, and that Hunter was in DC. He knew the people who had the juice, that was clear. And it worried me.

I went through the door into Archie's gym and saw him in his office. I went in and closed the door.

He said, "I saw what you've been driving. What happened, your whale have a guppy? Haw!" Arch was so happy with that little piece of wit he slapped the top of his desk. Pens and a paperweight bounced up in the air.

"It happens to be a loaner. Gets a gazillion miles per gallon. It's good for the environment."

Arch barked a laugh, "Ronny, don't give me that crap. You'd drive a tank if it was legal."

"Hey, I'm all for going green."

Arch said, "I know you use recycled paper and save aluminum cans and all that, but you've got this thing about what you drive. I think it's got to do with your –"

"That's enough. Stop right there."

Archie's eyes twinkled and he leaned back in his chair. "What's up?" I told him about Rakes' threat on Hondo. He said, "What do you need me to do?"

"You think you could keep him at your place for a while, not tell anyone?"

"You need help getting him here?"

"No, but I'll do it at night and come in through the back."

I'll be watching from there, say about nine?"

"That'll do."

I went to my office and called Hunter again. She didn't answer so I left a message on her voice mail telling her of Rakes' threats and for her to be careful. Then I called my insurance agent and got the news on what they would cover on my house. It was actually very fair and I told him so. The next step would be to find a contractor to clean the lot and rebuild my home. I figured that was for another day.

I had hours to go before kidnapping Hondo from the hospital, so I went into the storage room and rummaged through some unpacked boxes until I located the novel I picked up at a bookstore and had not read. I sat in my chair, propped my feet on the desk and opened it.

Talk about hard to put down, I almost decided to leave Hondo overnight so I could finish it, but finally gathered enough willpower to put it down at eight PM. I called the hospital and got Hondo. I told him about Rakes and my plan for him.

Hondo said, "Drive up to the front. I'll be there."

"You don't want some help escaping? Those nurses looked plenty tough to me."

"Right now they could take me in a fight, but I've got cunning on my side."

"Cunning who?"

"Meet me in front." He hung up and I went next door to borrow Archie's Corvette. If Rakes was going to chase me, I wasn't going to be in a Yugo this time.

**

I pulled to the front entrance and saw Hondo step out of the hedges still dressed in the hospital gown. He trotted to the Corvette and got into the passenger's seat.

I drove away and said, "That gown's open in the back. When you turned around it looked like a white globe with a crack in it."

Hondo rested his head on the seat and breathed hard, "It's kind of breezy on the nether regions." He coughed several times, sighed and closed his eyes.

We were back and in Archie's apartment in thirty minutes. Archie had the guest bedroom made for Hondo and gave up the Lazy-Boy recliner for him to sit in when we arrived.

"Thanks, Arch," I said.

He gave me shoo-away signs with his hands, "It's nothing."

I said, "Say, you know that purple drink you make, that super elixir? Maybe you can make some for Hondo every day, kind of get him on his feet."

Hondo pointed his finger at me from the recliner, "Don't make trouble. Don't listen to him Arch."

Archie said, "It's good stuff, you'll see. Get you back on your feet in no time."

Hondo shook his head and said, "I'm going to sleep."

Archie said to me, "Don't worry. I'll be with him at night, and I've got a friend named Waylon Lakes that'll be with him during the day."

"He getting out of the nursing home to come do this?"

"Very funny, whippersnapper."

"Can he handle trouble?"

Waylon's a Vietnam vet, tough guy whose first ten days in Nam were in the A Shau Valley at a little place called Dong Ap Bia, then it got worse after that. He can handle trouble."

I said, "He's in his sixties?"

"Uh-huh. Just now hitting his prime."

"He doesn't need me to bring him some Ensure or anything?"

"Har-har, funny guy. You tell that to Waylon. Now get out of here so Hondo can rest."

I went out the door and walked around the building to my office, thinking, did he call me a whippersnapper? I went inside and fiddled with papers and other items, then with curiosity still itching at me, I turned on the computer, popped up Google and typed in Ap Bia. After reading several of the items I figured Waylon probably could handle himself. I had heard of Ap Bia, but under its other name: Hamburger Hill.

After doodling on the internet for an hour, I got up and stretched, then walked outside. That's when I saw the Yugo.

It was parked ten spaces to the left of the office, with a note under the wiper. I read it under the lights of the parking lot.

Dear Mr. Baca, Thank you for saving me. I felt terrible leaving you like that, but I was so scared I just drove and drove. I am glad you are all right. I called the police and they told me. I am sorry, but I cannot stay in Los Angeles. I am too afraid. Please find my sister and cousins before they are hurt. I know you can and I don't believe anyone else is good enough or brave enough to do it. I will call you in a few days with a number.

Thank you,

Blanca.

PS The keys are on top of the left rear tire.

I got the keys and jangled them in my palm. Sometimes it's a burden being seen as a can-do guy.

**

The next morning Bond Meadows came into my office. She wore a skintight black Lycra dress that showed a lot of leg and a huge amount of cleavage, like something from Frederick's of Hollywood, the Whip Me, Whip Me section. Her lips were pinched tight and she said, "You are messing everything up and you're going to get hurt, do you realize that?"

"Everything? Like The Big Bang theory, the human genome, upside-down pineapple cake?"

"You think you're so funny. I'm serious, you could be hurt," she chewed on her lower lip, "And I wouldn't want that."

"It's a little late for warnings. Your omnisexual partner Carl already threatened me."

She came around the desk and put her hands on my shoulders, her face close, eyes sincere, "I know we had a few problems, but I can make it up – will make it up to you if you'll give me the chance." She moved her face closer and I could smell the expensive perfume coming from the dab she'd put between her breasts. Her lips parted for a kiss and I gently pushed her away.

"Nuh-uh," I said.

Bond surprised me by not getting angry. Her eyes teared up and she said, "If you could just give me a chance."

I said, "I'm going to find Bob Landman, and I'm going to find out what Rakes is up to. If you and Frank are involved, you'll go down with him. You have a chance right now. Take what you can and run, far away. It's the only warning I'll give you."

"I could please you in ways you've never imagined."

"The only way you could please me is by leaving."

Her eyes hardened. "I'm going to enjoy it when Carl gets his hands on you. Nobody can stand up to Carl."

I smiled at her and it seemed to make her angrier. She said, "I will tell him to make it especially painful. He is a big, powerful man, much bigger than you."

"I've got goosebumps from the thought. Now, please go."

She left, slamming the door as hard as she could. Ah, the women in my life. I tried to do other things but her perfume was there every time I breathed and images of her body ran through my thoughts. I went into the bathroom and took a long, cold shower.

I dressed for hiking, then went outside and drove away in the Yugo. I pulled into a store on the Sunset Strip that sold globes and maps and bought a topographical map of the area I wanted, then drove into Pacific Palisades and the start of the trail that Mickey showed us. It seemed like a long time ago.

I didn't have a bike but made good time. I reached the bluff where Hondo had scrambled around like a cliff monkey, then I went down the trail to where we found the undocumented Mexican women.

Past the oaks, there were no more paths, only game trails. I checked the topo map and started down the winding slope to the bottom of the canyon, then walked the canyon floor as it snaked northeast. The brush was thick in places, and I had to detour a dozen times. There was little breeze and the afternoon sun was heating the canyon bottom like a furnace. I walked another hour before rounding a long curve and the vista opened to a wider valley.

The area had opened up but the terrain was still rough, with large boulders and brush. I would have to weave my way through it. I hopped on a boulder and referred to the map, then saw the cave a half mile ahead. It was maybe ten feet above the canyon floor on the east side, the mouth showing clear as it caught the afternoon sun. A small thread of smoke came from a fire pit. Here was the answer to another piece of the puzzle left by Landman on his scrap of paper. It was indicated in small print letters, right at the edge of my topographical map. I had come to Chumash Cave.

I got to the entrance in ten minutes. The roof was black from ancient fires and the floor was dust and rocks. The cave went back about fifteen feet and from outside it had the shape of a half-opened eye, narrowing at both sides. The roof was twelve feet high at the center and followed the taper down to the corners. A ring of stones showed a fire pit where white ash still smoked. There were several blankets scattered about, along with opened cans of Ravioli, Rosarita refried beans and a trash sack full of Kataki's Gourmet Kobi Beef Jerky wrappers. A plastic jug still full of water was against the back wall. There were lots of tracks and flattened areas and I could see areas of dark spots scattered here and there, looking like someone had flicked paint off a paint brush. The spots were blood, still congealing. Someone had had the crap beaten out of them. I was no tracker like Hunter, but with all the dust it was easy to see there had been six or eight people in the cave and they were grouped with four having large prints and the other four with three sets of small prints and one average print. The blood spots were always near the average prints. The tracks showed everyone leaving the cave and going farther down the canyon. I noticed a crumpled paper under the edge of a boulder and picked it up. It was a topo map, but not the one I had. I looked around the borders until I saw the name of my topo. Great. It was the *next* map of the canyon, starting just past Chumash Cave. It showed a clear dirt road a half mile down canyon. I had walked maybe ten miles to get here, and if I'd looked at the very next map, I could have driven to within ten minutes of the place.

I was glad Hunter and Hondo weren't here, I'd never live it down. Jeez.

I studied the cave again and my eyes kept returning to the far left corner and a jumble of rocks. I walked to it and kicked one with my toe. There was no dust covering the flat stone. The others had a fine coating like sifted flour. I used my toe to lift the edge and saw a tiny piece of black plastic protruding from the earth like a blade of grass. I moved the rock and pulled on the plastic. It was a trash bag, but wouldn't come out. I dug with my hands and uncovered the bag enough to open the drawstring. Inside was a rolled up cloth the size of a basketball. I took it out and the first thing I noticed was the weight. I put the cloth on the ground and opened it.

It was treasure. Three items were inside. The first was an incredible egg, decorated with gold and jewels. I picked it up and opened it. Inside was an exquisite miniature carriage encrusted in precious stones and gold. I put the egg together and laid it down. Pictures don't do justice to a Faberge egg. The second item was a gold crucifix maybe eight inches high, with emeralds and rubies the size of my thumbnail covering the surface. The third was a fine chain gold necklace with a palm-sized pendant made of different colored diamonds. There were varying sizes of clear diamonds forming the outer ring, then a group of six marble-sized deep blue diamonds evenly spaced around the center piece, which was a canary yellow diamond the size of a walnut.

I sat on the ground and looked at the items on the cloth. Letting undocumented people transport something like this was a very risky play. It indicated to me these people were desperate, and the items obviously stolen. They must have lookouts at every Port of Entry and International airport in the country, I thought. There was a better chance bringing it in by using the undocumented than they would ever have trying to pass through Customs.

So, Bob Landman brings the undocumented aliens here to protect them and to hide out himself, then he hides the artifacts, and Rakes and his crew find them. They beat Bob up, but he won't talk, so Rakes takes all of them to some place safe where they can work on Landman and the women as long as they want until someone talks. Then they will kill everyone and dispose of the bodies, leave no witnesses.

I wrapped everything up in the cloth, put it back in the trash bag and slung it over my shoulder. I used the second topo map to take me to the dirt road. I followed it for four miles to pavement where I sat in the shade of a large boulder and called Archie on my cell phone to come pick me up.

Talk about *whine*, Archie went on so much he sounded like a seven-forty-seven. He finally relented but said he first had to help his thirty-two year old girlfriend finish her pelvic thrusts.

I didn't go there.

CHAPTER THIRTEEN

Archie took the turns in his Corvette as if he was competing at Le Mans. I held on and cinched the seatbelt a little tighter. The trash bag was between my feet on the floorboard.

"What's in the sack, you picking up aluminum cans along the road now that you're unemployed? Haw!"

"It's jewels from the last czar of Russia."

"Uh-huh. Boy, you just can't answer a question without being a smartass, can you?" He mumbled something else.

"What did you say?"

"I said I'll be glad when they get your four-wheeled tuna-mobile finished. You're closer to a normal human being when you have it to drive."

"It should be finished tomorrow."

"Good. Now really, what's in the sack?"

"Some things I found that might be evidence."

"Now see, wasn't that easier than making up wild stories?"

"Been a revelation. I'll do things this way from now on." Archie pulled up and parked by my Yugo with a satisfied smile on his tough brown face.

**

The first thing I did at the office was to put the jewels in our file cabinet and lock it. Holding millions of dollars in stolen jewelry causes a weight on your mind. My next move was to tell Hondo, and I went into Archie's apartment and met Waylon, who looks like Morgan Freeman with more gray hair. We talked for a while, then I went to the bedroom where Hondo was propped up with pillows and reading an Elmore Leonard paperback. I told him what I'd found and what I thought.

Hondo said, "You want to use the jewels as trading material, get Landman and the women in exchange for it."

"Yeah, I figured they'll bite."

"They'll try and kill you and take the jewels, is what they'll do. Then they'll kill Landman and the women so there are no witnesses."

"That's how I've got it figured, too."

"I'll just get my clothes," Hondo said and got out of bed. He might have wobbled a little, but it could have been my imagination.

"You can't go. You're weak as a kitten."

He put on his jeans and shirt, then his socks and shoes. "You don't have anybody else," he said. Hondo stood and leaned against the doorjamb. I think it was for support. He said, "Come on, it'll be legendary, like Wyatt and Doc, Butch and Sundance."

"Abbot and Costello," I said. Hondo grinned and started out the door. I followed him to our office, waiting for him as he caught his breath after every dozen steps.

We went inside and Hondo sat at his desk. "My legs are wobbly," he said.

I said, "What a pair, The Tumescent Detective and Noodle Man."

"Yeah, Bad Guys beware." Hondo looked around and said, "I wish Hunter was here."

"Me too, she can shoot."

"Shoot the ears off a flying gnat at a hundred yards."

"At night."

"Blindfolded."

I pulled the phone to me and said, "Might as well find them so we can start the ball."

Hondo leaned back in his chair, "We might as well," he said and closed his eyes.

I called the Caspian Diamond and they told me Mr. Rakes was not in and hadn't been all day. I tried Siberia next and got no answer. I said, "You think I'm getting the run-around?"

"Uh-huh. They don't want to be disturbed. Sure be easy just to tell the help to lie."

"At least it's not because of my personality."

"Don't bet on it," Hondo said.

I stood up, "I guess you're up for a drive, huh?"

Hondo got to his feet, went into the storage room and came out with a twelve gauge Remington pump. He racked a round into the chamber and fed another fat shell of buckshot into the magazine, "I am now," he said.

Hondo almost balked at going in the Yugo, but we finally got underway. I stopped at a convenience store and bought two quarts of Gatorade, some peanut M&Ms, and a pack of Tic-Tacs for good luck. We were ready for surveillance now.

We watched the Caspian Diamond for three hours and never saw a familiar face. I finally couldn't stand it anymore and told Hondo I was going inside. He patted the shotgun and said, "We'll be ready."

I opened the door and stepped into darkness and Lenny Kravitz singing *American Woman*. I let my eyes adjust before easing into the main room. A blond woman worked the pole in time to Lenny, moving her body in smooth undulations that made her seem boneless. I controlled my lecherous thoughts and walked to the bar. There was a different bartender, and none of the Russian thugs were in the audience or sitting on barstools. I ordered a beer, and over the next two songs maneuvered my way to the office door. It was closed with no light showing underneath. I leaned my back against it and turned so one ear was against the door.

I didn't know if that really worked, but it seemed like the thing to do. There was only silence. I hitched at my pants, turned to face the door, opened it and stepped in. I heard the bartender shout at me over the music as I closed the door behind me.

At the far end of the hallway was a door with EXIT stenciled across it in big red letters. Halfway down the hall on the right was another door. I opened it. This was an office, but no one was there. A notepad was on the center of the desk, and on an impulse, I put it inside my shirt.

I heard footsteps coming down the hall and I stepped out to meet them. "Where the heck's the bathroom?" I said.

**

Five minutes later, drained and refreshed, I left the club and drove away. Hondo complained about needing to pee and I told him to be a man and hold it.

I relented fifteen minutes later, and while he went into a McDonald's to use the restroom, I tried to find a pencil to shadow the empty page of the notepad. There wasn't anything in the Yugo and I didn't have anything in my pockets. Hondo returned with a small bag of french fries and got in the car.

"Couldn't use the bathroom without buying something, could you?"

"I feel guilty if I don't."

I asked him if he had a pencil and he snorted. I said, "Okay, just asking." I drove off and a few minutes later saw a Wal-Mart and pulled in. I bought a pencil and handed it to Hondo when I got back in the car.

He coughed and said, "What do you want me to do with it?" He looked tired. Being up this long was sapping what little strength he had.

I didn't want to let on I was worried, so I said, "Use your knife and sharpen it. We can't decode secret messages if it doesn't have a point."

He looked at me. "I left my knife in somebody's shoulder. I haven't had time to go get it."

I sighed, "I guess it's another job for me, huh? Boy, the load's getting heavy."

"I'm like the song."

I said, "What?"

"Like the song, I'm not heavy, I'm your brother. Go in the store and buy a pencil sharpener." Hondo was asleep when I returned and he didn't open his eyes until I started the engine.

When I drove away Hondo said, "You had to buy a Care Bears pencil sharpener?"

"It was the only one left." Hondo shook his head and sharpened the pencil. At the next stop, he stroked the side of the graphite point across the pad and ghost letters appeared.

I said, "What's it say?"

"Somebody with nice penmanship wrote this. There are just fragments of words, sentences. One says, *like Valdar* and another says…the first is a partial word that says, *-date Sarana*. There are some numbers, forty million, three million, twenty-two million something. They're stand alone, not like someone adding them or anything. That's all I can make out."

"Well, that was enlightening." I said.

"If catching bad guys was easy everybody would do it."

The traffic was moving well on Sunset and we reached Siberia in good time. I pulled into the vacant parking lot and noticed a sheet of typing paper taped to the front door. I had to walk over to read it: *Closed for renovation*. "That was quick," I said.

I put my ear to the door and heard nothing. I tried the knob but it was locked. Back in the Yugo, I told Hondo what the sign said. He nodded and pointed to the notepad, "I've looked at it some more and I think this first word is *liquidate*. If they're going to liquidate Sarana Corporation, then it would make sense that they shut down Siberia, or fix it up to sell. Either way it sounds like they're pulling the plug."

"Not without their last haul."

"Uh-huh. They make Landman or one of the women talk, tell them where it is, and when they have it..." He spread his hands.

"No more Landman, no more corporation, no more witnesses."

"Just millions in jewels and cash." Hondo coughed hard as he finished talking. I looked at his chest and saw a spot of red on the shirt.

Hondo wouldn't let me take him to the hospital, so I took him to Archie's and put him to bed. Arch was there and when I left, he was hovering over Hondo like a gruff old mother hen.

I went to the office and picked up one item, then drove into Beverly Hills and up to the front door of the Meadows mansion. There was no crawling over walls and hiding in leafy kangaroo pouches this time. I had to make a deal and fast or Landman and the others would be done for. I rang the doorbell and waited.

Frank Meadows answered the door and his jaw fell. "What the hell are you doing here?" He looked over his shoulder and hissed, "Rakes is here, you idiot. He'll take your head off if he sees you!"

Old Frank seemed worried and his face looked haggard, with pouches under his eyes and a nervous tic in one lid. I said, "Tell him I want to deal."

"Deal what?"

"Frank, be a good messenger and go get Rakes."

He hesitated, and I pushed past him. He said, "Hey!"

I walked down the long hallway and heard voices coming from a side room. I went through the double doors into a library that had floor to ceiling bookcases filled with books. Sitting in two large leather chairs were Carl and Bond. Snifters of amber liquid were on tables by each of their hands.

Frank pushed past me and said, "I told him not to come here."

Rakes stood up. His eyes were hot and he clenched and unclenched his fists. He growled, "Foot of hairsnake filth man valks to room of African cat. Gud is for me."

I shook my head and pointed first at him, then at me, "The message isn't getting through, Carl. You have to be able to *communicate* so the listener understands; otherwise, your threat doesn't have an impact. If they think the noises coming out of your mouth are just a cough or maybe you're asking them if they want an apple or something, it doesn't work. You'd be better off keeping a translator around. Now, are you trying to say I'm walking into a lion's den, is that it?"

Bond spoke from her chair, "Yes."

I kept my eyes on Carl and said, "I've got a proposition you might want to hear."

Bond said, "Let me hear it."

"You tell your monkey to sit down and we'll talk."

Bond said something to Carl in Russian and he said something back, then sat down.

I said, "Let's work a trade."

Bond said, "What do you think we have that you would want?"

"Oh, an Oscar caliber actor and a few pretty illegal alien women."

Bond sat silent, but observant. Carl said something to her in Russian. Bond said, "We have no one, you are mistaken."

I looked at Rakes, "I was in the canyon. I saw you take them, saw you beating Landman." It was a lie, but I thought it was time to bluff.

Carl and Bond conversed. Frank stood apart, useless as a stump. Bond said, "We do not have Landman or anyone else...but for curiosity's sake, if we did, what do you have to trade?"

"Well, assuming I did have something to trade, it might be a few things like this," I took the gold and jewel crucifix out of my shirt and held it at them as if they were vampires.

I could see Bond's eyes light up. Frank muttered, "By damn..." Carl smiled, reminding me of a Great White.

I said, "I want them back safe and sound. I'll give you this," I wiggled the cross, "And the other little trinkets when I get them."

Bond and Carl had their heads close and talked for several minutes while Frank and I stood. I said to Frank, "You are way out of your element here."

He bit at his lower lip, "You get old and scared, afraid to lose everything you worked for..."

"Get out."

"There's too much..."

"Walk away while you can."

Frank took a deep breath and looked at Bond as she talked to Rakes. His head tilted a little to the side and his mouth softened. I watched Frank's eyes fill, then he looked at me. "I can't," he said.

Rakes said, "Baca, ve say vhere the meet. Ve-tell-*you* how is to be for."

I looked at Bond and said, "You tell me, listening to him is giving me a headache." Rakes fumed.

Bond said, "As I said, we know nothing about where Landman is, or anything about illegal aliens. You're mistaken about what you saw." I didn't acknowledge anything. Bond continued, "But we will do what we can, and maybe we can locate these people for you. Why don't you bring the artifacts to the loading docks at San Pedro tomorrow at sundown. If we find them, we'll bring Landman and the others on our yacht and drop them with you on the docks. We'll keep them on the *Americas* until then, for safekeeping of course."

"Americas is the name of your boat?"

"It is a *yacht*," Bond said.

"Call me at the office and let me talk to Landman, then I'll come."

"I think we can arrange that," she said.

Rakes stood and pointed at the cross, "Leave it."

I held it out as if to ward him off and said, "Back, spawn of Satan!" He looked puzzled and mad. I said, "Didn't you ever watch Dracula movies?"

"Movies are for veemin and childs."

"You don't know what you're missing." I put the cross in my shirt.

He took a step forward and said, "Leave it."

"You get it when I get Landman."

"I take id from you."

I said, "You'd better bring your A-Game."

Bond spoke to Carl in Russian, then said to me, "We trust you. You may leave."

"Just what I planned to do," I said. I turned up my collar like a tough guy and walked out of the mansion with sweat trickling down the sides of my face.

I figured that little soirée would stop the beatings of Landman and the women, so I had a little time. There was a message on the answering machine when I got to the office, and I pushed Play as I opened a Coke. Bond's voice said, "We've located Mr. Landman and the women. Meet us tomorrow as we discussed." Click. Well, I wasn't going to let that go. I'd told them I wanted to speak to Landman, or no deal. I called the Meadows home and Bond answered.

"Meadows residence."

It's me. No deal."

"What?"

"You let me talk to Landman or it's off." There were some murmurs in the background.

Bond said, "Wait a moment, I'll put you on a three-way call." It took maybe a minute, then Bond said, "Okay Bob, talk."

Landman said, "This is Robert Landman."

I recognized the voice from a dozen movies. I said, "Are you sure it's you?"

He sounded tired, "Yes, I'm sure. I don't know you, but they say you're going to help us if I cooperate."

"I'm working on it." I heard his phone disconnect, then Bond was back on the line.

"Is that enough for you? We'll meet you at the dock for Dry Bulk shipments. It will be away from most eyes. Wait at the loading slip just north of the US Borax terminal, sundown tomorrow."

"You bet, sweetcakes."

"I could have been, you know," Bond said, then hung up.

I checked on Hondo, but he was asleep. It was four PM in LA, so Hunter's time was three hours later. I called her cell phone and got the recording. I left her a message to call me. I twiddled my thumbs, wrote and scribbled on a notepad, and was using a rubber band to shoot paper clips across the room at a bull's-eye superimposed on a photo of Osama Bin Laden.

I'd just bopped Osama on the beak when the phone rang.

"Deadeye Baca, Private Investigator."

"Baca, you change your name?" It was the body man at the auto repair shop. He said, "Well Deadeye, you got wheels again. I did it up special." He sounded proud. "You're gonna shit you'll like it so much. Come get it."

**

He was right, I almost did. I got out of the Yugo and stared as he stood by my truck, arms folded across his chest and smiling like a proud father. He said, "Pretty good, huh?"

"What did you *do*?"

"I put a little class on her, gave her some pride.

Won't be any others around LA like this baby."

I was speechless. There was my truck with a huge, black dorsal fin on the roof. The body man wiped his hands on a red rag and patted the top of the Ford. He said, "I got to looking at it and felt it was incomplete. I had this fifty-seven Chevy out back was just junk, and it came to me."

"It came to you," I said.

He nodded like I got it, "Yeah, take the fifty-seven's fin and weld it to the roof, lengthen and customize the shape and add some metal here and there, paint it black to match, and...tah-dahh."

My head hurt. "Can you take it off?" He looked like I'd slapped him. I said, "It looks uh, like nothing I've ever seen, something out of my dreams," *Nightmares* is what I was thinking, "But I work undercover a lot, and everybody'd recognize me this way."

He frowned, "I hadn't thought of that."

"I have to make a living," I shrugged as if I was sorry.

"I hate to." He rubbed his chin and thought for a good thirty seconds, "Okay, bring it by in a couple weeks. I'll take it off."

"Two weeks?"

"It's the best I can do. My customizing work is backed up."

"You can't slip me in?"

He shook his head, "I've got my ethics to think of."

"Well, can I drive the Yugo until then?"

"No can do. Somebody else is taking it this afternoon. They'll have it for a month." He smiled, "She's a starlet, got like forty first names, Mary Annie Billie Bobbi Ulysses Johnson, something like that. She was in that big teen slasher movie showed last month, said she's in a very turquoise mood and wants me to paint her Beemer turquoise and inlay the dash with silver and rhinestones. In the meantime she wanted to drive something people wouldn't pay attention to and I told her she could take the Yugo."

Well, she was right about that. I tried one more thing and pointed at the big fin, "Are you sure that's legal?"

"Yep. Had some CHPs drop in to make sure. They were so impressed they called their buddies to come by and take a look. Must have been twenty or so stop by in the last two days."

Great, my days of driving over the speed limit and whizzing through the pack was over. I imagined a trooper watching traffic coming at him on the freeway and seeing the black dorsal fin knifing through the cars like an orca chasing seals on a National Geographic special. Be hard to miss.

I surrendered, "Are the keys in it?"

"Yep. I'll send you the bill, no charge for the extras."

As I drove down the highway people in every vehicle within a quarter mile, coming and going stared with big eyes and often, open mouthed laughter. I sympathized with every zoo monkey I'd ever ogled.

It wasn't over when I pulled into the parking lot because Arch and his girlfriend were on the steps. Arch pointed, grabbed his stomach and laughed so hard he had to sit down. He sent his laughing girlfriend inside to tell everyone and before I could find an empty space, get out and run to my office, forty or fifty people came out and joined Arch. I parked and tried to remain dignified as I walked to my office. Once inside I pulled the shades and didn't answer the knocks on the door.

The knocking and hoots of laughter stopped after ten minutes or so. I waited another minute, then went out the door and into Archie's apartment. Waylon was there and gave me a nod. I asked, "Is he awake?"

"Yeah, I had to push him back in bed, tell him I'd give him an enema if he didn't behave."

"I'll bet that worked."

"Always does."

I went into the bedroom where Hondo was sitting up, reading *Macbeth*. He looked good, with color back in his face.

"Don't start talking like that," I pointed at the book.

He put it down, "I hadn't read Shakespeare in a while. It still holds up."

"Yeah, old Willie could write."

Hondo said, "What's up?" I told him about the upcoming trade. Hondo said, "You know where they're talking about?"

"I do. They'll come in by Angels Gate Lighthouse and pass under the Vincent Thomas Bridge, then through the turning basin and into the center channel. It's out of the way."

Hondo smiled, "That's to our advantage. How do you want to play it?"

"I'm going to call Deco Martinez."

Hondo nodded, "I can hardly wait."

CHAPTER FOURTEEN

I didn't sleep well. It was like pre-game jitters. The morning, though was perfect Southern California. No inversions were trapping the smog and the sky was clean and clear, with a slight breeze off the ocean that brought the smell of salt and fish and hints of faraway places.

Hondo came in the office's front door laughing so hard he couldn't make coffee. He wiped tears from his eyes, "Ohhh, nice *fin*," then started laughing again and had to sit down at his desk holding his chest.

"Go ahead, get it out of your system," I said. Hondo chuckled, wiped his eyes again and finally got some self-control. He looked almost back to normal, except for the dark circles under his eyes.

I said, "You must have bionic lungs. Nobody else could be near death one day and ready to go fifteen rounds two days later."

"Maybe four, no way fifteen. I guess I'm getting old."

"Oh sure. You still get carded at liquor stores."

He bit into a donut and said, "Probably just my clean living. Put some cream and sugar in my coffee will you?"

We talked to Hunter at mid morning and she told us about a spectacular theft within the last year of Russian jewels from the collections in Moscow. Interpol and the Soviet government were conducting a joint investigation. Total value of the stolen artifacts was over four hundred million dollars.

Hondo said, "Using that stuff for trading cards is risky."

"Uh-huh, but we told Mickey we'd find Landman."

"Yeah, I didn't mean it wasn't worth it, just that it's risky."

"Aren't you the one who told me 'Live on the edge every once in a while, feel a little adrenaline rush.'"

Hondo grinned and finished his coffee, "Yeah, that was me."

I said, "I thought it was."

**

Deco called right before noon and said he had taken care of things. To celebrate, Hondo and I went out to eat at James' Beach on Venice Boulevard. For a day like this, we sat outside and people-watched as we chowed down on some delicious peppered Mako. Afterward we walked along Venice Beach and talked about the sundown meeting. Every once in a while, I lost my train of thought as an exceptionally beautiful woman or two or three caught my attention. I tell you, some of those bikinis are so small these days.

We went back to the office an hour later and both of us took a nap. When we woke up, Hondo said, "This investigator work sure takes a lot of discipline."

"Hey," I said, "We do it by the book."

The rest of the afternoon, we cleaned our pistols and loitered around the office, reading books and magazines or turning the radio to different stations. Waiting is always the hardest part.

**

When it was time, we drove in Hondo's Mercedes to San Pedro and Los Angeles Harbor. The glowing sun was a finger's width above the horizon when we parked behind the enormous US Borax warehouse. We walked past it to the next loading dock. The smell of the sea was fresh and strong and sea gulls made their sounds and flew overhead. I looked up and saw their undersides turn glowing white as the feathers caught the sun.

Near the water's edge were several thousand stacked forty-pound bags of ammonium nitrate fertilizer being moved by a half dozen Hispanic men, with one driving a forklift. Another Hispanic man stood by a large piling at the water's edge, holding a fishing rod with one hand and watching the line where it entered the water. The other hand was at his side, a forty-ounce bottle of beer hanging from one finger inserted into the neck.

Somebody whistled from far off and the forklift driver turned his ball cap around so the bill pointed down the back of his neck.

"It's showtime," Hondo said. I could feel the sun warming my shirt and the heat settle into my skin. Small beads of sweat tickled my upper lip and I felt one drop run out of a sideburn and slide by my ear and down my neck. I glanced at Hondo but he wasn't sweating. He probably had a towel secreted on his person.

We could see into the turning basin and watched as a long, sleek white yacht angled toward us. Soon the sun was directly behind it, turning the water an orange red and making the yacht appear to be churning through an ocean of copper and blood.

Hondo and I stood forty or so feet from the dock's edge, with the workers and the pile of fertilizer on our right. The *Americas* came in and with the grace of a beautiful ship and a good captain, settled against the dock cushions. Two men hopped off and slipped ropes fore and aft around two old, rusted dock cleats. The Hispanic fisherman had to move a bit to his right to have his line clear the bow of the yacht.

A gangplank slid over to the dock and we watched people moving about on the *Americas* deck. Rakes crossed to the dock and I almost snorted at him. He was wearing a white, long-sleeved shirt open down the front, with an oversized collar and puffy sleeves, like something out of an old pirate movie. I figured he was a closet Fabio fan.

Bond and Frank were the next two off the yacht. The two men who tied off the boat moved to flank the others. I noticed one of them was missing the top half of an ear.

In my head things got very still. I could see everything in perfect detail, from Frank's twitching eye to the two hard nubs pushing out the front of Bond's silk blouse; hear every sound from the creak of the ropes to the lapping of the waves against the pilings underneath us.

The men working at the fertilizer sacks paid us no attention, and the forklift moved pallets of the stuff from back to front in a never-ending cycle some twenty feet on our right.

"You have de trade?" Rakes said.

I held up a plain green gym bag.

Rakes said, "Open."

I opened it, took out the egg, the crucifix and the necklace one by one, then put them back.

"Bring it to me."

"Nope."

Rakes said something in Russian and the two outside men started forward. Hondo made a tsk-tsk sound, pulled two Glock forty-fives from the back of his waistband, and let the pistols hang at his sides. "The man said, 'Nope'." Hondo glanced at me, "I get that translation right?" I nodded.

The men stopped and looked back at Rakes.

The men working the fertilizer glanced over, but didn't change anything they were doing. The fisherman yawned and took a pull off the forty, like he saw people carrying weapons in each hand every day.

Bond said, "Give him the jewels, Ronny. It's best if you do what he says."

"Nope."

Carl and Bond murmured to each other and Frank moved toward them, only to have Carl put his hand in Frank's chest and shove him away, hard. Frank staggered back five or six feet, his face flushing red. He stood there shifting weight from foot to foot in an awkward, antsy rhythm.

Bond went below deck and several minutes later we saw Landman and two small women appear. Their hands were tied behind them and even from here, I could see Landman's face had been worked over as bad as if Mike Tyson in his prime had pinned him in the corner.

Rakes said, "Dey are here. Now give chew-els to Carl."

"Nope," I said.

Hondo said to me, "You're just a little chatterbox today, aren't you."

Carl and Bond conferred some more, this time with Carl animated, swinging his arms and pointing at us. Bond touched his arm and he slapped her hand away. She sighed then turned to us and said, "So, we have a stalemate. We won't turn them over without the jewels, and you won't turn the jewels over without them. Do you have a suggestion?"

"In a minute. First, I want some things cleared up."

Bond said, "Go ahead."

"Frank and Carl were in on it from the first, when you hired us to find Bob. Your little scared act was to keep me off balance, and the play by Frank and Carl at my house when you were there was to reinforce that. Am I right so far?"

Carl and Bond conferred. Bond said, "You're right. We'd been searching for Bob, but it was as if he'd vanished. We asked around and heard you were very good, but that you were even better when you had an emotional attachment. So I used myself to pull you further in, with Frank and Carl pushing you and keeping you off balance so you wouldn't catch on."

I turned to Bob. "What made you take off?"

Bob looked at Carl and Bond then said, "They'd been using me as a patsy when I discovered what they were doing:

smuggling in undocumented women and stolen treasure taken from Moscow. I dug a little deeper and found the women were forced into nude dancing, prostitution and selling drugs, and the Romanov treasures were being sold on the black market to keep Americas Studios afloat.

"I was approached by an agent of the Russian government and told him I would help."

I said, "Valdar."

Bob nodded, "Yes. He was a legitimate artist, but also worked for the Russian authorities. I let him stay at my home in Malibu while we tried to dig further. When they found out, they killed him."

I asked Bond, "Where's Valdar's body?"

Carl answered for her, "Chum for Sharks."

Bond said, "I didn't know."

I asked Bob, "How did Deco fit in?"

"He's my friend. Valdar and I talked to him about the situation and we agreed to play along with Carl and the others until there was enough to hang them. But we tried to get too tricky."

I said, "Deco helped you save the women, didn't he?"

"Yes. We had been meeting at a motel where Carl and the others would bring the women and I would act as the mutual friend between them and Deco, whose reputation made him believable as someone who would buy women and farm them out to clubs. He was good and made the Russians see it as a beneficial thing, with him riding herd on the women after the Russians brought them in. Deco convinced them he could guarantee the women danced at the right clubs and didn't skip."

I said, "But you started intercepting the groups after they were dropped off."

Yes, after we found out at our last motel meeting that a Russian named Simon Mortay murdered one of the women at his club because she wouldn't prostitute herself. Deco took the two women at the motel and hid them in another state, then told the Russians they ran out on him. Deco and I talked it over and knew we couldn't let any more women die, so Deco found out the route and drop-off location and I gathered the last group, five women, and led them to a different place."

"Why on foot?"

"Because Carl's men were watching me by then, watching my cars and my house. It happened very fast and frankly was the only thing I could think of. I took them up a canyon to an area near the trail where I rode my bike. I felt it would be easy to keep watch on them that way and not be followed."

"And that's when Carl found out about Valdar."

Carl growled, "Yes. Ve take care of him."

Bob said, "I called Deco when I heard. We were going to get the women out of the canyon and to a place of safety, then we planned to hide out, too. I rode my bike, and figured to take the women out one by one, but I saw Carl and some others on my back trail, coming on dirt bikes. I left my bike and climbed down on foot. Two of the women weren't there but I couldn't wait, so I led the others away to a place I knew, Chumash Cave."

"There was a lot of food left there, so you'd planned on using it before and stocked the place?"

"Yes, as an alternate plan if I couldn't get them out on the bike. I did it in a hurry, grabbing whatever was at the house and taking it there. I drove and used a dirt road to get close, then walked in and cached the food. I drove back home and immediately got on my bike and went up the trail to the women."

I looked at Carl, "But you didn't throw his bike off the cliff until the next day."

Carl said, "Stupid Baca. Ve tink he return for pretty bike. Next day I know he runs. I throw bike from cliff."

I wagged my finger at him, "You should learn to control that temper."

Carl's voice turned icy. "Enough talk. De chew-els or I kill Landman."

I said, "Okay. Let someone neutral hold the bag until we trade."

"Who?"

I pointed to the forklift driver, who didn't notice. "I'll give him the bag to hold until we get the people, then you get the bag from him."

Bond and Carl talked again, arguing back and forth until Carl shook her by the shoulders so hard her head looked like a bobble-toy. He let Bond go and took a step toward us.

He pointed at the forklift driver, who again didn't notice, "Not to him," Carl said, then moved his finger to the fisherman, "To him. I tell him to vatch bag and I pay." He walked to the fisherman, who looked way, way up at Carl.

"That's not who I would have picked," I said to Hondo.

"Beauty is in the eye of the beholder..." Hondo said.

The fisherman nodded, put his rod down, zigzagged his way around several pallets of fertilizer to us, and held out his hand.

Pretty Boy winked as I put the bag in his hand, then he went back through the stacks to the rod, put the bag down by his leg, nodded to Carl and resumed fishing. The forklift moved near him and picked up a six-foot high pallet of fertilizer. Pretty Boy was obscured for several seconds before the driver backed the load to the far end of the pile. Carl watched to make sure the bag was still with the fisherman. It was.

Carl barked at Frank to go on board and get Landman and the others, but Meadows wasn't going to do it. He stood his ground with his fists clenched.

Bond said in a tired voice, "Frank, go ahead. Let's get this over with." Frank looked at her, then unclenched his hands and boarded. He started to untie them but Carl said, "No, leave them tied." Frank shot Carl a look, but that was all, then he followed Landman and the women up the gangplank and onto the dock.

At the same time, the forklift was bringing a pallet of fertilizer from the far back to the front. I saw Carl watch it, then I saw the change in his eyes. I thought, Uh-oh.

Carl roared a command in Russian and every eye on the Bad Guy's team got big and round.

Carl raced toward the fisherman.

Bond's mouth opened and she looked at the forklift. The two henchmen drew Berettas with each hand and aimed at Landman and the women.

The forklift driver gunned his machine and turned toward the two gunmen by the yacht.

The men working by the stacked fertilizer pulled Tech-nines and Mac-tens from thin air and started blazing away.

The fisherman dropped his rod, picked up the bag and backpedaled as fast as he could between the pallets, yelling, "Hey, hey, hey!"

Automatic and semi-automatic fire sent splinters flying from the docks and puffs of grainy fertilizer exploding from the sacks of fertilizer. Bond dropped to the dock and covered her head as Frank screamed, "Bond! Bond!"

Hondo fired what sounded like a hundred fast rounds from his Glocks right by my ear and knocked the two gunmen down. Me, I pulled my puny six shot revolver and ran toward Landman.

Bob Landman may have been a pretend hero in the movies, but there was real bravery in him, too. When the shooting started, he yelled for the women to run and he deliberately dropped behind them to keep his body between them and the Russian shooters. I raced by the women and behind

Landman to shield him and cut his ropes with my pocketknife. The shooting had started to fall off after Hondo knocked the two men down, but as I glanced at them and pushed Landman ahead of me, I saw the Russians rise.

I emptied my pistol at them and saw shirts jump with every shot. Hondo emptied both weapons. The Maravilla guys on the stack of fertilizer tossed their empty weapons aside and came forward with fists and knives. Hondo said, "Vests!"

I felt a bullet *zipp* by my face as one of the Russians fired. I pulled the trigger and heard the click. I yelled at Hondo, "*Now you say 'Vests'!*"

I glanced around and saw Carl catch the fisherman, and Pretty Boy tried to fight him, but Rakes simply ripped the bag from his hand, then grabbed Pretty Boy by an arm and his crotch and swung him like a hammer-thrower, sending him sailing over the top of the stack of fertilizer. Pretty Boy yelled, "I can't swim!" right before we heard the splash.

The forklift driver, Cuarenta, leaned out the driver's side to fire a Tech-nine around the stacked pallet as he drove toward the Russians. Cuarenta's bullets plunked into the yacht but not many rounds were finding their mark. It drew the Russians' attention away from me and Landman, though, and they concentrated their fire on the forklift.

I saw a round hit Cuarenta in the shoulder and another one caught the side of his head. He went limp and the forklift veered as his hand fell off the wheel. The forklift knocked a cleat into the air, crashed into the gang-plank and bounced off the dock and into the yacht at a crazy angle, trailing a stream of golden liquid from a ruptured fuel tank and spilling the sacks of fertilizer on the deck as the forklift careened on its side to land on top of them. A flying fifty-pound bag of ammonium nitrate knocked out Frank as he rushed toward Bond.

The momentum of the colliding forklift moved the boat away from the dock and the single rusted cleat gave way and dropped into the water, still attached to the line from the yacht.

Movement among the pallets caught my eye and I swung my attention that way in time to see Hondo and Carl facing each other.

A bullet tugged at my shirt and I saw the Russians aiming at me. Landman was beside me and I pushed him, "Run!" I said. I turned back.

Behind the Russians, on the yacht, I saw Cuarenta get to his knees, bloody head and all, and take his time with the Tech-nine. There was a flat sounding shot, one Russian's hair flew up on the back of his head, and he fell face down. The other turned and the Tech-nine clicked. The Russian raised his pistol and *it* clicked. Cuarenta jumped at the Russian and they went down in a heap on the dock, rolling and slugging and kicking.

Frank staggered to his feet, still yelling for Bond.

I shouted at Landman "Get the women behind that big warehouse," then ran toward Hondo as the other Maravillas went to help Cuarenta and Pretty Boy.

I heard Carl as I raced to the pallets.

Carl said, "You vish to try Carl, hah? Carl break you like stick of shit."

Hondo said, "Prove it."

Carl grinned and came at him. Hondo hit him so hard Carl's feet came off the ground and he hit on his back, but was up in a second.

"Grin some more," Hondo said.

Carl wasn't grinning now. He was mad clear through. I reached them and ran to attack Carl from the left and he snapped the fastest side-kick at my head that I'd ever seen. I partially dodged it, but enough connected that I went down in a floppy heap, still conscious and able to see and hear, but motor functions were short-circuited. I saw Hondo come at him and Carl focused his blows on Hondo's chest and back. He grappled with Hondo and used his knees like a Thai boxer, driving devastating pneumatic thrusts of knee and thigh into Hondo's chest and sides as he held him.

Hondo broke free and staggered back. Blood stained his shirtfront and back, and a thin red trickle from his mouth that looked way too bright. I tried to stand up on noodle legs and felt like my head was floating on a stick body two inches wide and ten feet tall.

Rakes closed in for the kill and Hondo waited until Carl swung his right hand, then Hondo grasped Carl's arm at the wrist and elbow and used the Russian's own momentum to take them both over. Hondo continued in a roll that brought him up first, with one knee centered on the forearm between his two hands.

He broke Carl's forearm like you would break a stick. I staggered toward them as Carl screamed from the pain and drove his left fist into the red spot on Hondo's shirt.

Hondo went over backward and didn't move. Carl rolled to his feet and cradled the right arm to his stomach. He picked up the green bag and turned to go.

I tackled him around the shoulders and held on as he ran toward the *Americas*. He stopped long enough to elbow me loose and followed with a hard kick that sent me backpedalling until Bond caught me. Cuarenta and another Maravilla stood between Carl and the drifting yacht, but they might as well have been children trying to stop a lion. Two swift, savage kicks left them both unconscious on the dock. Carl never even put down the gym bag.

I tried to pull away from Bond but she held me tight and said, "No, he'll kill you."

The *Americas* was sideways to the dock, but twenty feet away and moving farther every few seconds. I saw Frank regain his feet on the yacht and look around. Carl looked at the *Americas* and tossed the gym bag underhanded so that it landed on the deck. Carl then backed up about fifteen steps, stuck his broken arm in his shirt and ran forward.

Rakes leaped at the edge of the dock and sailed high through the air to land in a stumbling fall on the deck that knocked him and Frank down. I heard Carl yelling and cursing in pain. You didn't need to translate Russian to know that fall hurt.

Chato had Hondo's arm over his shoulder as they walked over to stand beside me. Bond stepped away and looked at the yacht. Carl stood up, then Frank, who still looked woozy. Carl held up the bag and said, "I vin, the chew-els vill cause me riches!"

Frank's voice wavered, "Bond...."

I glanced at her and saw she was looking at the bag. She said in a soft, tired voice, "He doesn't have them, does he." She said it like a statement.

"Nope."

"How did you know who he would ask to hold the bag?"

"I didn't. The fake one was on the forklift, the side you couldn't see. It went back and forth in front of everyone, so it didn't matter who was picked, they would have time to exchange the bags."

Bond nodded, "Clever."

"World's Most Clever Detective."

She smiled a sad smile and we both looked at the boat.

Carl laughed and waved the bag, then he put it on the overturned forklift and reached inside.

His laughter stopped as he drew out a coffee can full of sand with the lid duct taped on and dozens of Happy Face stickers stuck on the can. Carl reached in again and drew out one of those black globe fortune telling eight-balls you give kids who then ask it questions and turn it over to read the messages that floated up like: *Ask again later*, or *Outcome Doubtful*. He looked desperate as he reached inside the bag. He lifted out two pink bubblegum cigars taped together to form a cross. I'd also glued colored M&M's to it. His eyes widened, like he couldn't believe it. He reached in a last time and pulled out a rubber chicken.

I yelled, "Spend it wisely!" We could hear sirens in the distance. Pretty Boy came up with the other Maravillas behind him and handed me the real gym bag. I held it up and let Rakes see it.

Carl's face twisted and he began to look around on the boat, disappearing from sight as he went below deck. Frank cried and looked at us, holding his hand out to Bond. When Rakes appeared again, he had a Bery pistol in his hand. He raised it to fire and yelled, "I burn you, Baca!"

Frank yelled, "No!" and pulled Carl's arm down as the Russian fired. The two struggled as tongues of flame and black oily smoke spread in the burning diesel around the forklift. The last thing I saw was Carl pulling Frank in front of him and backing away from the fire.

The yacht exploded in a gigantic ball of flame and noise. The concussion was so strong it knocked all of us off our feet. Debris and burning ash rained down on us and I heard the different pitched metallic *wangs* and *bonks* as various sized pieces hit the roof of the Borax warehouse behind us. There were also horn honks and faint yells and whistles and applause coming from the bridge. They thought we were making a movie. Only in LA.

Pretty Boy stood up and looked where the *Americas* had been. There was a little fire on the water and bubbles and ash, but nothing else. He said, "Man, you guys know how to take care of trouble."

Bond stood beside him and said, "My husband was on that boat."

Pretty Boy shrugged and said, "He should have found somebody else to hang out with, *Chulita*. Man's gotta walk the walk if he's gonna talk the talk." Pretty Boy took another look at her and said, "Say, you gonna be needing a man now, uh? Fine looking lady like you, maybe I can fix you up."

I said, "Trust me, the Maravillas don't need that kind of trouble."

Pretty Boy winked at me, "Whatever you say, Holmes." We could hear sirens in the distance. They were coming our way.

I said, "You guys take off, Hondo and I'll take care of it." I took Hondo's arm from Chato and put it over my shoulder.

Hondo looked at me and said, "I still ain't heavy..."

I said, "Don't kid yourself. You are." Pretty Boy and the others lined up and gave Hondo and me big *abrazos*, then left, laughing and comparing wounds. They were a tough bunch of guys.

Bond said, "What are you going to do with me?"

"Let you tell your story to the authorities. Bob and the women will tell theirs, Hondo and I ours, and you can be last. I understand there's a lot of international interest in this," I held up the gym bag, "and all of them will get a shot at you."

She stroked my arm, "Couldn't you let me go, for old time's sake?"

"I can't, for any kind of sake." I looked at Hondo, "What exactly *is* a sake, anyhow?"

The first police sedans came into view and I saw Landman and the women talking to them. "I wouldn't worry," I told Bond, "You'll look good in prison colors."

The officers motioned us to them and we walked slowly, with me holding up Hondo, and Bond pacing beside us in silence. Bob helped hold Hondo when we reached them, and the officers put Bond in cuffs.

We were busy with everything else when Bob said, "I'm sorry about your car." Hondo and I looked past the police cruisers and saw the mangled forklift on top of Hondo's Mercedes. The Mercedes was maybe two feet high.

I said, "Look at the bright side; you've always wanted a compact." Hondo punched me on the leg because that was as high as he could lift his arm. The paramedics took him before he could hit me again.

**

That night and the next two days were a crazy mix of statements to law enforcement, Immigration, the Russian Consular office, every news and television reporter in the area, CNN, and Univision. Hondo even got a call from People magazine wanting Hondo and I to appear on their cover as *The Sexiest Private Detectives Alive.* Hondo told them we'd do it right after we saw *The Sexiest Dead Private Detectives* issue on the shelves. I'd kind of wanted to do it, but Hondo was still being cranky because he was back in the hospital. The same nurses he skipped out on were watching him like hawks this time.

Bob Landman came by to thank us and to talk. He turned out to be a warm and genuine person, and we both liked him. He asked us about the case, about Mickey -- we talked a lot about Mickey, and then we mentioned Hunter. He asked a number of questions about how the government treated her because of her helping us.

Bob also did us some favors without us asking. Some people say politicians can get the biggest things taken care of, but an A-list actor isn't far behind. He made a few calls at noon the next day and by mid-afternoon Hondo and I were licensed PI's again and licensed to carry. We received phone calls apologizing for the mistake and assurances that it would never happen again. That evening we were told they had recovered Frank Meadows' body, but found no trace of Carl Rakes and assumed the explosion had blown him apart.

We got a call from Hunter the second morning. She was laughing and saying not only was she exonerated, but they encouraged her to "continue her productive relationship with friends of the motion picture industry". DreamWorks had also contacted her to act as a consultant for *Ninety Notches*.

Bob had a good sense of humor, too and didn't try to hide his beat up puss from the cameras. He was witty and self-deprecating to the news cameras and got a lucrative benefit from it. Gillette contacted him and offered a low seven-figure contract for a one-minute commercial with him using their new Mach razor to shave his bruised and cut face. They said it would show how gentle-yet-close-cutting their Mach was. They were sure it would rocket sales, but the trick was they had to film right now, before Bob's cuts and bruises faded.

So on the third day I was with Bob and a film crew shooting the commercial on the Sunset Strip. Bob hired me as a PA -- Personal Assistant, something I'd never been before. I'd had to drive there in Shamu, fin and all and that got some comments and stares. But finally, we got down to work. Bob told me all I had to do was hang out on the set and look smug. I told him I thought I could do that. The pay was good and Bob said I could call Hondo in the hospital from the set and torment him about it.

The location on Sunset was maybe thirty yards east of Siberia, still closed for renovations according to the sign.

It was mid-afternoon and I watched them put shaving cream on Bob's face for the first take as I talked to a cute-as-a-button brunette from Salinas who was employed as a Best Boy. The name was misleading because she would never, ever be confused for a boy. I had her chuckling and trying to be quiet on the set when the first take was ready and "Action" shouted.

Bob talked into the camera with his face covered in shaving cream. He held up the razor and told of its merits and technological design. That's when a movement coming from the right caught my eye and my first thought was, I didn't know they had a monster in this commercial.

The figure rushing onto the set wore a charred and torn white long-sleeve shirt and oil-smeared pants, but the face was what shocked me. One half of the head was a black, scorched scalp and face with a milky white eye bulging from the socket. The other half was a mane of long, tangled dirty blond hair, and a snarling face with one blue eye. One arm was tied to his stomach with dirty rope. Dark burns showed through the tears in the shirt, and then I recognized the tattoos, and the good half of the face.

Carl Rakes had risen from the dead.

I ran forward and pulled my new Glock .45 as Carl grabbed Bob from behind. He had Bob around the neck with his good arm, and his hand held a long shard of glass against the side of Bob's throat.

Carl backed away, "Dah, you film dis. You see Carl take de shid actor and carve him away. You vill see, you vill see. Carl vill triumph!"

I pointed the Glock, "Let him go, Carl. It's over."

"You shoot, Damn Baca. Go ahead, kill de actor, I not care!"

It was too risky. Carl backed down the Sunset Strip dragging Bob backward as cars slowed and watched. One of them hissed at us, "What's the name of this movie? Looks good." He gave us a thumbs up and drove down the street.

I stalked Carl with the film crew following me. Carl reached the front door of Siberia and opened it. So, that's where he'd been since the explosion. Somehow, he'd made it all the way here. He closed the door and locked it, then I heard a heavy weight slide against the door.

I said, "Call Nine One One, tell them what's happening," and I put my Glock in the shoulder holster to wait for the negotiating team to arrive. The only problem was, Carl wasn't going to give us that much time.

Everyone heard Bob's scream. It was long and high-pitched, full of pain. People behind me moaned, "Oh God, oh God..."

I ran past them to Shamu and started her up, then spun tires as I backed into the Sunset Strip amid squealing rubber and honking horns. The set people saw what I was doing and they ran into traffic, stopping cars. I pulled my Glock and put it on the seat by me as I circled the big Ford across the lanes in an arc and came around with the grill and dorsal fin headed straight for Siberia's front door.

I held onto the wheel as Shamu burst through the door and careened across the floor. I caught a glimpse of Carl standing in the middle of the dance floor holding Bob. Shamu was still motoring and I rammed the bar, knocking it into splinters, then felt the big iron-pipe bumper smack hard into the rack of aqua-lung thingees below the barrel of secret ingredients and everything exploded into gray snow and hissing smoke.

I felt beside me, but couldn't find the Glock. I searched the floorboard and under the seat, groping frantically. I grabbed change, an air freshener, a half-full box of magnums and a fly swatter, but couldn't find the pistol. I heard Bob grunt in pain, so I hopped out of the door and straight into a nightmare. There was a gray snowstorm inside Siberia.

It took me a second to realize the aqua-lung thingees had ruptured and exploded, blasting the Tunguska's secret ingredients into the air like movie snow. The tanks hissed, shooting vapor into the air like a dozen fire extinguishers. The flakes of Tunguska were whirling and swirling like a heavy blizzard. I had an inch of it on my hair and clothes and the flakes were so thick I couldn't help breathing it in. My entire body inside and out was tingling and hot-cold. My eyes watered and burned. I felt like I'd inhaled half the comet.

I heard coughing and walked toward the noise, but didn't make them out until I felt the edge of the dance floor with my toe. Bob was on his knees and Carl towered over him like a colossus. I stepped onto the dance floor, ready to take Rakes on if it would give Bob time to escape.

Rakes made a funny noise, like a snort and a gurgle at the same time. I stepped closer and saw he was holding his own throat with his good hand and his face changed colors as I watched.

Bob crawled toward me and I helped him to his feet. We both looked at Carl. The Russian shook his head back and forth and foam leaked out of the corners of his mouth like he'd eaten a handful of alka-seltzers.

He looked at us. His one good eye was as red as a cut tomato and the lids were swelling. He gasped, "Breathe...Help."

I didn't know about Bob, but *I* wasn't going to help him. We watched Carl drop to his knees and roll on his side, his lungs wheezing. His breath whistled in different octaves as he thrashed around trying to take in air, and the notes were as loud as a kid's plastic flute. In another minute, he rolled on his back, let out one small sigh and was still. The flakes covered him in a gray shroud until he looked like a fresh-made paper mache mummy.

Bob still had shaving cream on his face, but it was thick with flakes. I pointed at it and he wiped it off with his shirttail, then we walked outside to the cheers of the set people and forty or fifty Japanese tourists, each with three or four cameras around their necks and another one in their hands as they snapped away.

The police arrived ten minutes later and we again answered questions, but Bob was a professional and he cut the statements short and told them he had an obligation to fulfill and they could take all the statements they wanted after filming had wrapped. They said okay and let us walk away. A-list actors, I tell you.

They cleaned Bob up like new, but I was too tired and told them I'd get through this and clean up at my office. We moved a block down Sunset and set up again. The shoot went perfect and Bob did twenty-two takes, each one a little different and each one I thought was perfect. At the wrap I had the cutie-from-Salinas' phone number and got a ride home from Bob. I called on Bob's car phone as he drove and told the body shop repairman where to find my truck. He laughed when he hung up.

I shook Bob's hand when he dropped me off and he said he'd stay in touch. The hospital had released Hondo, and he was at the office. He, Arch, and Waylon were waiting inside when I opened the door. They all pointed at the thick crust of gray stuff on my head and clothes.

Arch said, "Haw! Worst case of dandruff I ever saw."

"You need to work on your routine, Arch, it's not funny." Well, that brought another round of hoots from both Archie and Waylon.

Hondo leaned back in his chair and said, "We saw it on the news. They filmed it all and even played the 'Jaws' theme when you drove Shamu in a circle and crashed through the door."

Waylon said, "Yeah, you guys must be pretty important because they broke into the middle of a Bonanza rerun to tell us about it."

Archie slapped his thigh and snickered. "They don't do that for just anybody."

I went to my desk and plopped into the chair, sending a cloud of gray dust and flakes into the air. In a couple of seconds, all three of them were sneezing and rubbing their eyes.

I put my hands behind my head, "It's good to be back," I said.

-###-

Thanks for reading *BACA,* the first novel in the Ronny Baca Series. I hope you enjoyed it.

Reviews help other readers find books. I appreciate all reviews, and every one matters.

The second novel in the Ronny Baca series, *L.A. WOMAN,* will be available this summer.